Above the flood, up on the counter, a color caught my eye. Bright green. It was Alisa's letter to C. S. Lewis—maybe forgotten. Or maybe she'd been too scared to ask for it back. I remembered how pale she'd looked that morning—all little and skinny in a dirty sweatshirt, with her eyes full of tears—and it just killed me. It occurred to me that what I'd just said to Douglas was probably the hugest lie I'd ever told anyone in my life. Because things weren't okay. They weren't okay at all.

ALSO AVAILABLE IN LAUREL-LEAF BOOKS:

ANGELS ON THE ROOF, *Martha Moore*
UNDER THE MERMAID ANGEL, *Martha Moore*
KISSING DOORKNOBS, *Terry Spencer Hesser*
WHIRLIGIG, *Paul Fleischman*
RADIANCE DESCENDING, *Paula Fox*
THIN ICE, *Marsha Qualey*
KINSHIP, *Trudy Krisher*
THE WAR IN GEORGIA, *Jerrie Oughton*
LIFE IN THE FAT LANE, *Cherie Bennett*
THE SQUIRE'S TALE, *Gerald Morris*

A Door Near Here

Heather Quarles

Published by
Dell Laurel-Leaf
an imprint of
Random House Children's Books
a division of Random House, Inc.
1540 Broadway
New York, New York 10036

ISBN: 0-440-22761-5

RL: 5.8

Reprinted by arrangement with Delacorte Press

Printed in the United States of America

January 2000

10 9 8 7 6 5 4 3 2 1

OPM

For Cynthie and Geoff
with all my love;
and for everyone who showed
us the way to Narnia

Chapter One

I was right in the middle of making a tomato sandwich, with orange guts all over my fingers, when my youngest sister, Alisa, marched into the kitchen, climbed up next to me on a tall wooden stool, and handed me the letter. I didn't even read it right away—just clasped it between the heels of my two hands and tossed it over to the only corner of the kitchen counter that wasn't covered with lunch bags and bread crumbs. How was I supposed to know it was the beginning of the end of everything, that stupid letter? It didn't look like anything dramatic at all; in fact, it was written on Kermit the Frog stationery. Besides, I had about eight hundred thousand other things on my mind that morning.

"Can you proofread that before I go to school?" Alisa asked me, watching her envelope slide to the edge of the marble countertop. "I need to have it spelled right for language arts." Alisa was in third grade. She's the quietest kid in our family, and very nice for her age, but oblivious when it comes to things like interrupting people who are busy.

I'd overslept by more than an hour. I was trying to memorize chemistry formulas for a test third period while I cut six tomato sandwiches into triangles, wrapped them in plastic, and stuffed them into brown paper bags—two for me, two for my brother, Douglas, one for my sister Tracey, and one for Alisa. The school buses were coming in twenty minutes, my hair wasn't brushed, the kitchen was in a state of chaos, and I kept tripping on Douglas, who was lying on the linoleum floor in pajamas with his head under the sink, trying to fix a leaky pipe. I was not in the mood for Alisa.

"Hold on," I told her, tripping over Douglas's legs. "Just wait a minute." I was rolling up the sleeves of my school uniform—too late because the cuffs had already dragged through the tomato juice and turned orange. "Douglas, will you *move*?" I nudged Douglas lightly with my foot, but he didn't budge. I kicked him harder, and he inched himself over to the right a little.

Alisa stayed where she was on the stool, swinging her legs. "I need to have it spelled right for school," she said again. "It's a letter to C. S. Lewis. It's supposed to be to your favorite author." She wasn't whining; she never whines. But I knew she was going to sit right there and repeat herself in a reasonable voice until she got what she needed. That's the way Alisa operates.

"Just hold *on,* will you?" I snapped. "What are you, deaf all of a sudden? I'll read it when I'm finished."

Alisa's shoulders jumped a little. She stopped swinging her legs, wrapped her arms around her rib cage, and sighed. Her eyes stayed fastened on the envelope.

"Katherine," said Douglas from under the sink, "turn on the water for a second. I want to see if it's still leaking."

I exhaled, laid the knife down on the counter, and

wrenched the faucet on. Water spewed out all around the edges, and I ground it back off. "Yes," I told him through my teeth, "it's still leaking. Just forget it, Douglas—you can mess with it after school." I picked the knife back up and began savagely cutting the rest of the sandwiches in half, keeping one eye on the digital clock over the stove. Eighteen minutes till the school buses arrived. We couldn't miss them—there was no one to drive us to school if we did.

"I've almost got it," mumbled Douglas.

Douglas was only fourteen then—he's one year younger than me—but he was a genius about fixing things. He fixed our VCR when it started eating tapes, and the smoke detector, and Alisa's radio. So when the faucet started leaking and he said he could fix it before school, I believed him. That was a mistake. Douglas is a genius about appliances, but he's stupid about everyday things like not missing the school bus.

I reached for the last of the sandwiches, grabbed the edges of the Wonder bread with one hand and the knife handle with the other, and stabbed across the middle. The blade slit straight down the middle of the bread and into the skin between my index finger and thumb. Dropping the knife, I stuck my hand automatically into my mouth, sucked the bloody slice, and was surprised how little it stung. Then tomato juice seeped into the cut, and it felt like someone had rammed a stake through my hand. "Shit!"

"What's the matter?" asked Douglas.

"Shit. *Shit.*" I shook my hand as hard as I could to numb the pain, then paused to look at the damage—a long red stripe, like a paper cut. I stuck it under the cold water faucet but this time nothing came out. Since I couldn't think of anything else to do, I swore again even louder, and threw the knife down into the sink as hard as I could.

"You cut your hand," observed Alisa from the stool. "You're bleeding."

"I *know.*" I stuck my hand back in my mouth and sucked, glaring down at Douglas, who still wasn't moving.

Alisa slid off the stool and came over to me. Her big blue eyes were full of concern, and her hair was lifted by static electricity so her bangs floated over her forehead like an orange halo. As she tugged my hand down to where she could see it, I noticed that she was dressed in the same jeans and sky-blue sweatshirt she'd been wearing for the last three days. It occurred to me that her teacher might notice something like that . . . might call the house to see what was wrong.

Retrieving my hand, I leaned over and spat into the sink. "Go change your clothes," I told her, irritated. "You can't wear those—they're dirty."

Alisa's eyes filled up with tears. "*All* my clothes are dirty," she whispered.

"Well, find some different dirty ones, then—you can't wear those. And hurry up—your bus is gonna be here in seventeen minutes." I grabbed the end of the paper towel roll over the sink, tugged off a chain of three, and wrapped them around my hand like a bandage. "Douglas," I said. "Hey. *Douglas!*" I kicked him again as Alisa fled from the kitchen, her socks skating over the linoleum floor.

"What?"

"Get out of there and go get dressed. It's eight-twenty-three."

There was a deep gurgling sound from under the sink, and then a metallic squeak. For a second I thought he'd fixed it. But then I heard a slurping sound, like bubbles draining from a bathtub. Douglas lunged up to a squatting position and I barely jumped out of his way before a rush of foamy drain water came spewing out everywhere—all over the pots and pans in the cabinet and out onto the floor in big, slimy rivers.

"Douglas!" I shrieked, climbing up onto the kitchen stool. "Turn that off!"

His face was wet, and his long hair, which was tied back with a bandanna, was beginning to drip. He leaned forward into the cabinet and fumbled with something under the sink. "Okay," he said, clearing his throat. "Okay. Hold on a minute."

Deep, smelly puddles of water were crawling across the kitchen at an alarming speed. "Turn it *off,*" I commanded again, trying to stay calm. "Just turn it off. I'm serious, Douglas. You're gonna flood the whole stupid house."

"Wait." I heard another creak, then a splintering crack, and the water started spraying out much harder than before, ricocheting off the cabinet door. Douglas stepped backward and rocked up on his skinny legs, wiping his face with his hands. "We need the main valve," he said. His hand went up to the back of his head. "Do you know where it is?"

I stared at him from the stool, hoping he was joking. "How should *I* know where it is, Douglas? You're the genius." Water spat against his legs and leaked down to the floor. It looked like fresh water now, I noticed—not drain water anymore.

"We need to shut off the main valve," he said again.

Our sister Tracey slammed into the kitchen with a towel turban wrapped around her head and another towel fastened tightly under her armpits. "What's going on?" she demanded between clenched teeth. "The shower's not working right. What in the hell are you guys *doing*?" Except for the pink fluffy towels, Tracey looked like a tall, tan stick figure, or a swimsuit model. She was thirteen. She still had strap marks on her shoulders, and it was halfway through October. She made me sick.

"What do you think?" I snapped. "Playing in the sprinkler. Indoors. Moron."

"The pipe broke," said Douglas.

"Well, *fix* it," said Tracey, her voice rising. "I have to get ready for school. I still have conditioner in my bangs."

I glanced at Douglas, who didn't say anything, and then down at the floor, which was now completely flooded end-to-end with water, filmy brown gunk, and half-chewed vegetables swirling around in tiny currents. Then a strange thing happened, which had begun happening to me more and more often in those days. My brain altered slightly. I could feel all my stressed-out energy grow taut, like a rubber band, and then loop around into an organized knot. I felt very calm, but borderline crazy at the same time, and I knew exactly what we should do. I got even bossier than usual. It was like a measured power surge or something.

I ordered Tracey to go grab some towels from the linen closet. She hesitated, so I grabbed the knife out of the sink and slammed it flat down on the counter for emphasis. *"Move!"* I snapped. I must have looked insane, because Tracey wasn't usually afraid of me, but she ran. Then I laid the knife down carefully on the counter and glanced at the clock. Fourteen minutes. "Where's the main valve?" I asked Douglas.

"I don't know."

"Well, you better find it . . . *now,* before the floor caves in." I climbed down off the stool and winced as my socks sank into the putrid water.

"Mom might know where it is," Douglas said hesitantly, looking pale under his freckles. He didn't move.

I glared at him. "Are you volunteering to go upstairs and ask her?"

Douglas turned even paler. "I can't go upstairs like *this.*"

"*I'm* not asking her," said Tracey from the doorway, with her hands full of towels.

"Well, neither am I," I said. "Just find it. Where is it—under the sink somewhere?" I grabbed the towels from Tracey, and she stepped primly back onto the carpet, away from the water.

"No," Douglas faltered. "Probably . . . maybe in the cellar."

"Then go *look,*" I growled. My blood pressure was soaring, I could tell. I thought I was probably on the verge of a heart attack or an aneurysm or a stroke, which *does* sometimes happen to teenagers—not usually, but occasionally. I'd read about that in a magazine recently.

Douglas clattered down the stairs. I braced the cabinet door shut with my foot, but that didn't stop the water from slithering through the cracks, laced with trails of mayonnaise and other miscellaneous scum. Tracey wrinkled her nose. "It's going to stain the carpet if it spreads," she said in a voice that was almost triumphant. "Mom's going to kill you when she gets up." Then she turned around and stalked off to her bedroom to finish getting ready for school.

" 'When' she gets up," I muttered. "*If* she gets up. What makes you think she's *getting* up?" I hurled some towels across the room to where the linoleum met the living room carpet, hoping to make a barrier and stop the flood from spreading, but I doubted it would do any good. I wondered how long we had until the wood rotted through and the floor collapsed.

"Katherine?"

Alisa appeared in the doorway again—this time in a dirty

pink sweatshirt. Her sneakers were tied carefully, and her bangs were smoothed down over her forehead, but she still looked messy—pale and exhausted. There were dark circles under her eyes, which I hadn't noticed before. They looked kind of scary on someone who was only eight. "I changed my clothes," she whispered, wide-eyed.

I kicked the kitchen stool closer to the doorway. "Sit on that," I ordered. "Stay out of the water."

Mutely she climbed up and sat, legs dangling.

I splashed across the kitchen to the cellar stairs and yelled down to Douglas, "Did you find it?"

"No." He sounded like he was almost crying.

"Shit," I breathed. "Shit shit shit."

I knew then that I would have to go upstairs and ask my mother. *I'd* have to do it because Tracey and Douglas wouldn't, and Alisa couldn't. I yanked my wet socks off, hurled them at the floor, and stomped up the stairs. I stopped stomping when I got to the second floor, and walked more carefully. I didn't feel as bossy anymore. I made myself walk softer and softer until, by the time I got to my mom's room, I was barely breathing and my power surge was gone. Just a little crackling static was left over, and it didn't make me feel anything besides shaky, like when you drink too much coffee.

Her door was shut and locked, as usual.

"Mommy?" I called softly, knocking. Then louder, "Mom?"

No answer.

Crouching down outside the door, I lifted the edge of the hall carpet to uncover a bobby pin, which we'd hidden there. Bobby pins would open any locked door in our house; Douglas and I had learned this in childhood, back when we used to spy on Tracey. In those old days, I wouldn't have believed it if someone had told me I'd be using the bobby pin trick on my mother. But times change, I guess.

Fitting the pin into the hole under the knob, I popped the lock and pushed the door open, trying not to let it creak. Then I stood still a minute, waiting for my eyes to adjust to the dark and see across the room to where my mother was lying under a lump of embroidered quilts. The shades were drawn, and the room looked sort of brown and shadowy. Everything stank like alcohol and bad breath, and her feet were sticking out from under the covers.

"Mom?"

She didn't move. Trying not to inhale the smell, I took a few steps toward the bed, very slowly, till I could see what was on her nightstand. There was a bottle of sherry with only about an inch of liquid in the bottom, a cracked Coca-Cola glass half full, three tubes of lip gloss, and a soup bowl with most of the soup still in it. Stopping to calculate, I counted two nights and two days since I'd brought that soup upstairs. She hardly ate anything anymore.

I poked her shoulder. "Mom. Mommy." She lay still as a doll, so I poked her again. "*Mom.* Wake up, I have to ask you something. Really quick, and then I'll leave."

"Goway," she breathed into the pillows.

Careful not to step on any of the empty bottles near my feet, I reached out to push her shoulder again, but she slapped my hand away with a force that encouraged me. I wondered if maybe she was starting to get better. A little bit of her hair was sticking out from the top of the quilt—blond and wavy like Tracey's—and if I only looked at that part of the picture, I could almost pretend she was fine. Just taking a nap or something.

"Mom, please listen. It won't take long. Just one thing and then I'll go away."

Slowly she raised herself to her elbows and squinted at me sideways, through her hair. Then she gasped, suddenly sounding afraid. "Who is it? Who's there?"

"It's Katherine."

"Who? What time is it?"

"Eight-thirty . . . in the morning." *Ten minutes till the school buses.* "Look, I just need to ask, do you know where the main water valve is? Douglas is trying to fix the sink."

She scowled at me like I was one of the gutted earthworms on the microscope slides in the science lab. "Katherine?" she said finally.

"Yes."

She dropped her head back down to the pillows. "Go away, I'm sick. Leave me alone, all of you." She rolled over to face the wall. Then she turned and sat up, leaning slowly to the left and staring at the night table until her eyes focused on the bottle of sherry. Her face was mottled by pillow creases. I couldn't stand to look at her swollen eyes, so I concentrated only on her hair, which was golden. Perfectly golden, like it always had been . . . for years and years, before her face had changed.

I decided to give it one more try. "The main valve, Mom. The main water valve? Where is it—in the basement?"

Her eyes suddenly focused blearily on my face, and I stepped out of the way because I thought she might try to slap me again. But she didn't. She started to snicker instead, which made the hair on my arms prickle.

"In the base . . . ment?" she echoed, shaking her head. "What are you talking about? Ask your *father* where it is—he's the one who wanted the stupid . . . house." She lifted the bottle of sherry and emptied the contents into the glass, sending it spinning in crazy circles on its base. She watched until it stopped teetering, then she gave a strange giggle and let the bottle fall to the carpet.

"Mom, Dad lives in Michigan. He left ten *years* ago."

She stopped laughing and swallowed. "Well, tell me something I don't already know. You little brat."

Right then Douglas stuck his head in the door. "Katherine," he whispered, "we found it. It's fixed. It's off." Then he shut the door again, too quickly so it made a slamming noise.

I backed toward the door, keeping my eyes on my mother. "Okay," I said. "Sorry. We found it, Mom. You can go back to sleep."

But Mom was suddenly moving quicker than I would have thought possible. She stood up, glass in hand, and leaned too far over to the left. "You kids get out of my bed, my . . . room." Her eyes were unfocused, looking crazily everywhere. "My *God,* can't you even let me rest in peace?"

She took a step toward me, but her foot got caught in the quilts tangled around her legs and she lurched forward, grabbing empty air with one hand and the tablecloth on the nightstand with two fingers of the other. Automatically I reached for her, and barely caught the weight of her body before she fell. Her fingers gripped my wrists, and her chin slammed into my shoulder. For a minute I thought we were both going to fall, but I pushed her body upright as hard as I could, and, hugging each other, we rocked back into a standing position as the night table turned over with a loud crash. She stumbled backward and sat on the bed, staring at me.

For a few seconds neither one of us said anything, and then my mom started to cry. "I spilled my drink," she said.

I looked down to where the glass had rolled onto the

carpet in a wet red-brown stain. The glass hadn't broken, but something else had—probably the lightbulb from the bedside lamp. "That's okay," I told her. "I'll clean it up."

"No." She was sobbing now, her face crumpled like Alisa's. "Just go away."

"Mommy . . ." My throat was starting to tighten. "I'll clean it up—it'll only take a minute."

She lay down in the bed and pulled the lopsided covers up over her face like a little kid. I turned toward the bathroom to get some paper towels and a dustpan, but then I heard her scream in a horrible voice, *"Just go away!"*

I didn't turn around, because I didn't want to see her face. I just left.

On my way back downstairs, I saw that the hall clock said 8:41, but it didn't matter because I didn't care anymore if I went to school or not. I didn't feel like doing anything anymore, except maybe sleeping for a long time. My hand still stung, and even my arms and legs were tired, like I'd been swimming.

Douglas met me in the foyer in his school uniform. His tie was lopsided, and his hair was still wet. "A-Alisa left on her bus," he stammered. "Ours is out there now. Tracey went out, but . . . the water in the kitchen. I didn't know if I should . . . she told the driver to wait—"

"Just go," I interrupted. "I'll clean it up. I want to stay home anyway."

He hesitated. He looked like a rabbit trapped in the headlights, unsure of which way to run, so I put my hand on his arm and gave him a push. "Go. Really."

"What about later? We have to meet Dad and Ophelia, remember?"

I grimaced. My dad and my stepmother were in town, visiting from Michigan. We'd arranged to meet them at a restaurant, but I'd totally forgotten about it. "Well," I said, "we'll have to go *meet* them, then, won't we?" I wasn't angry at Douglas, but my voice sounded like I was.

Douglas still didn't move. "How are we going to get there?"

"We'll take the bus. It's only five stops. Now get out of here—everything's okay."

"It is?" His eyes moved past me, up the stairs to my mother's room.

"Yeah. It's *okay,* Douglas. Run."

He ran. I followed him to the doorway and watched as he bolted through the leaves in our front yard—skinny and fast, with his backpack swinging off one hand in a graceful arc. Once he was up the steps, the school bus closed its doors, lurched, and sputtered away, taking Tracey to St. Agnes (which is our wretched, awful Episcopal girls' school) and Douglas to St. Luke's (the equally wretched brother school of St. Agnes). When the bus turned the corner, I sighed and walked back to the kitchen.

Above the flood, up on the counter, a color caught my eye. Bright green. It was Alisa's letter to C. S. Lewis—maybe forgotten. Or maybe she'd been too scared to ask for it back. I remembered how pale she'd looked that morning—all little and skinny in a dirty sweatshirt, with her eyes full of tears—and it just killed me. It occurred to me that what I'd just said to Douglas was probably the hugest lie I'd ever told anyone in my life. Because things weren't okay. They weren't okay at all.

Chapter Two

By the time I'd found a Band-Aid for my hand, soaked up most of the flood, loaded the soggy towels into laundry baskets, and mopped, it was practically ten-thirty and I hadn't heard a sound from my mother, so I figured she wasn't going to get up. That wasn't exactly surprising since she'd been in bed for the last five weeks, ever since she'd lost her job. Truthfully, I was beginning to wonder if she was *ever* going to get up again, and what we were going to do if she didn't. We needed a plan for that. I needed to think.

I think much better when I'm smoking, so I changed into jeans and an old flannel shirt, tucked Alisa's C. S. Lewis letter carefully into my backpack, and banged out into the cool air of the backyard. As soon as I got out in the sunlight, I felt better. Slinging my backpack over my shoulder, I crossed the lawn and climbed the wooden tree-ladder up to our old tree house, which is where Tracey, Douglas, and I always go when we want a cigarette.

Now, before you start thinking I'm trashy or stupid or

something, I just want to say that I'm *aware* smoking is a terrible habit. Just for the record, I get practically straight As and I'm a moderately health-conscious person. I've seen all the ads from the Surgeon General about the million diseases it gives you, and how it's supposedly not cool, and it makes you look ugly, and everything else. With how much I read, I'd have to be really dumb to miss the point. The problem is, I started when I was thirteen because for some reason, everybody at Episcopal or Catholic school just *does*. You can't escape it. And once you start, you can't stop unless you have the willpower of Jesus Christ himself.

I've never figured out what the connection is, exactly, between going to religious schools and smoking—but I have two theories. Number one is that everyone feels compelled because we're forced to wear these dumb blazers and maroon plaid skirts every day (the guys have to wear blazers and maroon plaid ties). Smoking, we hope, will let people on the outside know we're not prudes but unwilling victims of an oppressive system that makes us wear prudish clothes. Theory number two is that all the pressure and rules get us so stressed out, we turn to unhealthy addictions to avoid hypertension (which I'm worried that I have already). I don't know. All I know is my father went to religious prep schools and he smoked like a fiend for most of his life, until he finally went to a hypnotist and quit. Now Douglas, Tracey, and I go to religious prep schools (because my father says we have to, and he pays the tuition on top of our regular child support) and *we* all smoke.

Alisa is the only nonsmoker in the family. Granted, she's just a little kid, but I seriously doubt she'll ever start because she's been lecturing the rest of us about quitting since she was four. Also, addictions are supposed to be hereditary, and Alisa won't inherit my dad's addiction, because my dad isn't

Alisa's father. She was born two years after my parents got divorced. I have no idea who Alisa's biological father is—I don't think my mother even knows—but whoever he is, chances are he never smoked nearly as much as my dad.

Once I'd opened the windows in the tree house and gotten some air blowing through, I sat down on a pile of folded blankets in the corner. Pulling a pack of cigarettes, a lighter, and a Coke out from under this plastic Snoopy playhouse-thing that's been kicking around up there for years, I leaned back against the wall and took several deep breaths to lower my adrenaline level. Then I lit a cigarette, drank my Coke, and made a list of things to do that day. (That may sound impossible to you—to drink, smoke, and write all at the same time. But it's not if you're ambidextrous—which I am.) This was my list:

1. *Proofread Alisa's letter*
2. *Do the laundry*
3. *Write in my notebooks*
4. *See how much food we have left and how much money Douglas has*
5. *Figure out what to do about Mom*
6. *Figure out a plan in general*
7. *Get ready for Dad and Ophelia*
8. *Find Alisa something to eat and to do while we're at dinner*
9. *Tell Douglas to buy more cigarettes for the tree house*

I looked at the list for a minute, trying to think whether I'd left anything out. It irritated me that there were only nine things. Nine is an unfinished number. After another minute I wrote hesitantly: *10. Study extra for chemistry test.* But then I thought, *Yeah, right,* so I crossed that out and just left it at nine. When I was finished, I felt much better about the day. (If you ever get stressed, you should try making a list of all the things you have to get done. I read that in *Mother's Magazine* once, and it's true that it actually lowers your heart rate.)

Unzipping my backpack, I pulled out Alisa's letter, which was beginning to look a little worse for wear. The green envelope was bent in half. It said on the outside: *"To C. S. Lewis the athor"* so the first thing I did was erase *athor* and write *author,* as neatly as I could while still making it look like Alisa's handwriting.

In case you haven't heard of him, C. S. Lewis is a famous children's author who wrote about an imaginary land called Narnia. Alisa is crazy about his books. She's read each of them about fifteen times—and even when she's not reading, she drags them around the house with her the way some kids drag a baby blanket. I remember starting the first one—*The Lion, the Witch and the Wardrobe*—when I was in fourth grade, but the first thing that happened was this kid from England stepped through the back of a wardrobe into a magic forest full of talking animals and dwarves. I could tell right away it was going to be a fairy tale, so I didn't finish. I never could get into fairy tales. Even when I was little, I only liked to read stuff that was realistic, which is the opposite of Alisa. (Not that I think it's bad she has a good imagination. I'm actually hoping it's a sign she'll turn out intelligent like me and Douglas, instead of stupid and shallow like Tracey.)

I opened the envelope and unfolded the stationery inside. On the top Alisa had drawn a lion and a unicorn head in colored pencil. The lion, labeled *Aslan,* was pretty good, but the unicorn's snout was too short so it looked more like a sheep with a horn. The letter started, "Dear CS."

I lit another cigarette and skimmed down the page.

Dear CS,

I like your books about Narnia. I read them all the time from the librerry. I don't have them because books are expensiv and my mom lost her job. But they are the best books I ever read. Another thing, I can tell you did not make them up because no one could make up espeshially about Aslan, so I know they are true. I was wondering if you could tell me where a secret door is from here to Narnia. I won't tell anyone and I will not notify the news people, so no one will think your crazy. I need to go to Narnia very bad, I think someone there can help my mom, she is sick.

Love, Alisa Donavan

PS. I know your books are about England but I live in America near the Washington Monument. I need to know a door near here because I have no money to buy a plain ticket.

Well, that letter was about the most depressing thing I'd ever read. I read it twice, and then I put it down because I was so sad, I felt a little sick. I remembered how Alisa had looked that morning before the bus came—how anxious she'd been about her letter, and how I'd snapped at her about her clothes being dirty. My eyes started to hurt like I had a headache behind my eyeballs, which is the closest I ever get to crying.

This is why: For one thing, I was almost sure C. S. Lewis

was dead. It was pretty pathetic to think of Alisa worshipping this guy's books to the point of hoping they were true, then finally getting up the nerve to ask him where the secret door to Narnia was, and having him turn out to be dead—probably dead for a hundred years.

For another thing, Alisa had mentioned my mom being "sick" in the letter. You're probably thinking, *Of course she did,* because most normal people *would* mention it if their mom was drunk in bed for five weeks, even if they were too little to know what drunk is. But the thing is, I was kind of hoping Alisa hadn't noticed.

See, this wasn't the first time my mom had gone on a drinking-sleeping binge for a bunch of days in a row. It was just the longest—because before, she'd always had a job to worry about. And even when Mom *was* up and sober, she was practically never around. She'd worked sixty hours a week ever since Alisa was a baby, so we hardly ever saw her on weekdays. Up until she got fired, she practically lived at Sheldon's Ad, Inc., which is an advertising agency in the city. The earliest she ever got home was eight, which is half an hour before Alisa's bedtime, and then she almost always went back out on a date with one of her millions of boyfriends. (She's gorgeous, my mom. She hardly ever eats because she thinks she's fat, but she isn't. She has perfect skin and marble-green eyes.) Sometimes she slept over wherever she had gone and just called the next morning about what to make for breakfast. So we never really relied on her being around—at least Tracey and Douglas and I didn't.

Douglas and I did all the housework and stuff. Pretty much all my mother ever did for us was buy groceries. Once in a while, she'd cook—not main dishes but desserts. Every couple of weeks, she'd get inspired. She'd say she was channeling Julia Child and talk in a weird duck voice while she made really good, complicated recipes, like lemon chiffon pie and peach cobbler. She made great peach cobbler. We loved those nights so much, we'd all cancel our plans and sit around in the kitchen watching her, laughing at her jokes, inhaling the smell of hot peaches and looking at how beautiful she was.

Even though she earned money, Mom herself was always saying that if it wasn't for Dad's child-support checks we'd all go down the tubes. That fact really pissed her off, which is why she worked so many hours to try to get promoted, and why it especially sucked when she got fired by her boss and ex-boyfriend, Sheldon, "for having one lousy beer on the job." That was all she talked about for the rest of the summer, which was extremely annoying. She bought a ton of new clothes, went around job hunting, got all these rejection letters. Then, finally one day in September, she just climbed into bed with her sherry and told us she wouldn't take any phone calls. She hadn't gotten up since, except for a couple of times to drive to the liquor store and buy more sherry.

My mom is an alcoholic, in case you haven't figured that out by now. She has all the signs. I've read a million magazine articles on the subject, so when she started drinking so much and missing work, I knew what was going on and I explained the whole thing to Douglas and Tracey. It didn't take a rocket scientist to figure it out. But Alisa didn't know—she just thought our mom was sick. And as I sat there in the tree house thinking about it, I decided we probably should have explained it to her . . . exactly what was wrong with Mom.

A gust of wind tore through the tree house then, almost yanking Alisa's letter out of my fingers, and the whole tree house swayed back and forth in the branches, making all the floorboards creak. I looked at my watch and saw that it was almost eleven-thirty, which meant only four more hours of freedom, so I stuck the empty Coke can and the rest of the cigarettes back under the Snoopy playhouse-thing and climbed through the trapdoor, and down the ladder to the grass.

On the way down, I missed the last rung of the ladder and almost fell over backward. I guess I wasn't used to smoking so much in the morning. Grabbing the ladder for balance, I leaned against it for a while, feeling dizzy and watching the red leaves blowing around our backyard in the cold wind. Puffy clouds gusted over the sky, throwing moving shadows across the lawn. A crow swooped down near me and landed on top of a beet-red sapling, squawking and making the tree sway crazily under his weight. He bobbed a few times, pounded his wings against the air, and took off for a higher tree, using the branch as a springboard.

For some reason, once the dizziness passed I started to feel better again. I decided that once my dad and stepmother's visit was out of the way, Tracey, Douglas, and I should have a meeting. We needed a more organized way to deal with Alisa and Mom—and life in general. Also, sometime soon, I'd take Alisa to the library and break it to her as nicely as possible about C. S. Lewis being dead. In the meantime, I'd do the laundry and then take a nap before we had to go meet Dad and Ophelia at the restaurant. And maybe everything would be okay.

When I got inside, I tiptoed up the stairs to my mom's room and knocked. "Mom? Are you awake? Do you want any breakfast or anything?"

There was no answer, so I turned the knob as softly as I could and looked in. She was burrowed under her quilts again, making no noise at all. A sunbeam was slanting through the blinds and making the bed shine like a bright island in the middle of the dark room. The reek was overwhelming. I stayed there watching until I finally saw the quilts rise and fall a little so I knew she was still breathing. Then I shut the door.

On the way down to the laundry room, I happened to see one of Alisa's Narnia books lying at the edge of the stairs. I picked it up and looked at the cover. The front had a painting of a beautiful golden lion against a green background. He was staring into the eyes of a witch who seemed to be made of ice. Behind the witch was a pack of demons and red-eyed werewolves with claws and swords. Behind the lion was a group of four children. The children didn't look scared, so I guessed the lion must be protecting them. I flipped the book over and skimmed down the back cover till I found a little blurb about the author. *Clive Staples Lewis,* it said, *1898–1963.*

I didn't read the rest of it—just shook my head and tossed the book back down onto the floor. I was right; he was dead.

Chapter Three

My dad and stepmother were practically half an hour late meeting us at the restaurant. That was fine with me. Our father only visited us once or twice a year, and I looked forward to it about as much as you look forward to getting plaque scraped at the dentist's. At first Douglas, Tracey, and I waited around in the bar, but after about fifteen minutes we couldn't take the jazz music anymore, so we went outside and sat on a bench near the entrance.

Tracey didn't talk to me or Douglas while we waited. She just calmly picked lint off her blue lamb's-wool sweater. After a while she took a nail file out of her purse and started edging her fingernails.

Douglas kept chattering at me till I wanted to kill him. Douglas is normally a fairly quiet person, but when he's nervous you can't shut him up to save your life.

"Dad and Ophelia are on their way to Hawaii after this," he told me, drumming a stick against the side of the bench. "They're flying straight from Washington. Dad's speaking at a conference there—some Dental Association thing."

"Oh."

"They're staying at a beachfront resort. They rented a Jaguar to drive while they're on the island."

"Yeah, you told me already. Listen, Douglas—you too, Tracey—if Dad or Ophelia ask how Mom's doing, just say fine, okay? Her problems are none of their business."

Tracey didn't look up, but I knew she'd heard me. Douglas shrugged.

"Okay," he said. "Dad rented a boat, too. They're staying a whole month."

I turned to look at him. "The conference lasts a month?" I said. "What are they going to 'conference' about? There's only thirty-two teeth in the human mouth."

Douglas stopped drumming and gave me a funny look. "The conference is three days," he said. "They're staying for a month of vacation."

I rolled my eyes and looked back out at the parking lot. "Whatever," I said, shaking my head. "I don't really care what they do."

I was five years old the day my dad left my mother and took off to live with Ophelia in Michigan. (Her name really is Ophelia, can you believe that?) She and my father have two kids—a son named Chandler and a baby girl named Miranda. Back when my father moved out, they didn't have any children, of course. I only knew who Ophelia was because she used to sit at the front desk of my dad's dental practice, and she gave me free purple toothbrushes when I went in for checkups. (That was a big deal at the time because they don't give kids candy at dentists' offices; they give them toothbrushes. The purple ones are very hard to come by, since purple is the favorite color of eighty percent of people under nine.) I used to hold the toothbrush handle up to my eye and squint so everything looked like it was underwater in sparkling grape Kool-Aid—including Ophelia.

Anyway, one day when I was five, Douglas was four, and Tracey was three, my dad took us all out to dinner at the Washington House of Gourmet Hamburgers. He bought us junior meals with Shirley Temple drinks and paper umbrella prizes. When we finished eating, he told us he was moving far away with Ophelia, the toothbrush lady—not because he didn't love *us,* but because he loved *her* so much more than Mommy. He said he made a mistake when he married Mommy, that grown-ups make mistakes too, but not to worry that he thought *we* were mistakes because he loved all three of us very much. Then he drove us back to the house and dropped us off on the front steps, and we didn't hear from him again until three years later—when he mailed us an invitation to his and Ophelia's wedding.

My mom yelled and swore and drank for three weeks after that. I still remember it. It was the first time I ever saw her drunk. Even though I didn't know what drunk was at the time, I knew something was different. She started serving popcorn for dinner every night, for one thing. In the evenings she'd sit down at the kitchen table with Tracey, Douglas, and me, and while we ate our popcorn, she'd tell us what a dirt-eating worm our father was, and drink sherry and cry. I kept thinking I would cry too but instead I just kept getting that headache behind my eyes. And ever since then, for almost ten years, I have never cried again for any reason. I'm not sure whether that should worry me or not.

"Is that them?" said Douglas, watching anxiously as a gray Jeep with tinted windows turned into the parking lot.

I sighed. I wished I had a quarter so I could call Alisa and make sure she was doing okay at home. "How should I know, Douglas?" I said. "Does it look like them?"

"He said he bought a Jeep."

"Half the world has Jeeps," said Tracey.

"Anyway, they flew here from Michigan," I said. "Whatever car they have is rented."

We all kept watching the gray Jeep, though. It looked like the kind of car my dad would rent, if he got to choose what kind he wanted. It pulled into a space at the far end of the parking lot, and after a few minutes a woman with long, straight black hair got out of the passenger side. It was Ophelia, all right. Her hairstyle hadn't changed in the ten years I'd known her. The driver's door opened and my dad got out too. He was wearing a polo shirt, and his hair looked grayer than when we'd seen him at Christmas.

Douglas stood up and waved. "Dad!" he called. "Hey, Dad! We're over here!"

Dinner that night was one of the most exhausting meals I've ever sat through in my entire life. For one thing, the Washington House of Gourmet Hamburgers is a very crowded and trendy place. It's my father's all-time favorite restaurant in the world. Each hamburger is named after some politician or famous dead person who used to live around Washington. Like, for instance, if they had a peanut butter burger it would be named for Jimmy Carter because he's a peanut farmer. (There isn't really a peanut butter burger, but that's the idea.)

The waitress seated us at a round table smack in the middle of the restaurant, so we were surrounded by loud, laughing people on all sides and we had to practically scream to hear each other. Ophelia had brought about a million pictures of their kids, which she insisted on passing around the table—one at a time—while we were eating. After a while the table felt like some kind of revolving Fotomat merry-go-round in the noisiest corner of hell.

My father seemed a lot more nervous than he usually was when he took us out to dinner—probably because he had Ophelia with him. Normally when he came through Washington on business trips he was alone, and we only had to deal with Ophelia when we visited them in Michigan. (That was every other Christmas and Thanksgiving, which I thought was plenty of time to spend with the woman who seduced your father and ruined your mother's life.) He ordered coffee with his dinner, and made the waitress refill his cup about nineteen times. He also sat so close to Ophelia, they might as well have shared a chair, and he held her hand throughout the entire meal—which was embarrassing in itself, considering they're both middle-aged.

"Where are Chandler and Miranda?" Douglas asked my dad. "Aren't you taking them with you to Hawaii?"

Dad and Ophelia laughed. Ophelia has perfect, pearly teeth like a mouthwash commercial.

"It's past their bedtime," said my dad. "We left them with Ophelia's friend Lynnea in Georgetown."

"We were over at Lynnea's earlier," said Ophelia, leaning forward and speaking loudly so we could hear. "She's crazy about the babies. She was my roommate in grad school . . ." She looked at my dad. "God! Was that *nine* years ago?" She flipped her hair back, and her ceramic bead earrings rocked.

Twelve, I thought, doing the math in my head. *At least.*

"Lynnea was the one who got me the job working at your dad's office," said Ophelia. "If it wasn't for her, we never would have met!"

There was a long pause after she said that. Someone at the bar turned the music off and the football game on, so the restaurant got less noisy. That was a relief, at least.

My father leaned back and cleared his throat. "How's your mother doing?"

Tracey and Douglas both looked at me.

"Fine," I said quickly, hoping I sounded nonchalant. "Great. She's at work all the time . . . you know, like usual."

Douglas squirmed.

"Good," said Dad. "That's great. How's Alissa?"

"Fine," I said, sitting up straighter. "She's in third grade now. She's really smart, though—she acts a lot older than eight. She loves to read." After a second, I added, "Her name is pronounced A-*leez*-a, not A-*liss*-a."

"Mmm," he grunted. Over at the sports bar, there was a collective shout. The Redskins must have scored or something. "The Skins are doing pretty well this season, huh, Douglas?"

Douglas nodded enthusiastically.

"How's St. Luke's team this year?"

"Uh . . . pretty good so far, I think!"

I stabbed a French fry. Douglas had no idea how St. Lukes' football team was doing. Douglas liked science-fiction books, Dungeons & Dragons, and music. The only sport he remotely enjoyed was cross-country, because he was naturally fast and he liked the woods. But my father didn't know any of that, and Douglas was willing to talk football all night if it meant Dad would pay ten minutes of attention.

While Douglas tried desperately to make conversation about extracurricular activities and classes at St. Luke's, my father put his arm around Ophelia's shoulders and played with the ends of her hair. He said "Uh-huh" and "That's great" at appropriate times, but his eyes kept darting back to the television over the bar. I could tell he wasn't paying attention, which made me want to kill him—or else kill Douglas for trying so hard.

After a while Ophelia smiled across the table at me and Tracey. "St. Agnes and St. Luke's seem like wonderful schools," she remarked.

I wondered what that was supposed to mean. Probably that we were supposed to feel eternally indebted to my father for paying our tuition to snotty prep schools we'd never asked to attend in the first place.

"Have you seen the uniforms?" Tracey asked her. "They're beige-and-brown plaid. They're the most hideous-looking uniforms of any school in Washington."

My dad shot Tracey an uneasy look, but Ophelia burst into delighted, musical laughter, which was extremely irritating. "I thought the brochure said 'cranberry and cream.' "

"Yeah, well—they're not," Tracey answered, looking from Ophelia to Dad. "Whoever wrote that must be color-blind. They're like . . . *rust* color."

Ophelia's laughter turned to coughing.

"Hey, babe?" My dad put his hand on Ophelia's back. "Is the smoke here bothering you? I can get the waitress to move us to another table."

I looked around the restaurant. Nobody was smoking anywhere near us.

"I'm fine, honey," she said, squeezing his arm. She took a sip of her water and swallowed. When her eyes stopped watering, my dad leaned forward and they kissed. They really were a step beyond nauseating.

"You sure brought a lot of pictures," I said, attempting to bring them back to reality. I started sifting through the pile of photographs. On top there was one of Chandler and Miranda together on a carousel—obviously posed. "Did you take this?" I asked Dad.

He chuckled awkwardly. "Ophelia's the photographer in the family, Kath. I'm just a clumsy dental surgeon."

Ophelia leaned forward to see which picture I was looking at. "Oh, *I* took that one. Do you like it? I thought of using it for a Christmas card. It's really sweet of Miranda."

I examined the picture critically. Miranda looked exactly like Tracey as a baby—blond and curly-headed, with a juice mustache and her arms thrown out to embrace the world. Chandler sat behind her, gripping the merry-go-round pole with both hands and looking terrified.

"Chandler looks a little tense," I remarked.

Ophelia laughed again. "Exactly," she said. "That's exactly what Chandler's *like.* And Miranda's just the opposite—she's a ray of sunshine. Your dad's always singing that song to her—you know that one, 'You Are My Sunshine'?"

We knew it. It had been my dad's special song for Tracey, back when she was a toddler. I glanced at Tracey, but she had no expression on her face. She held her salad fork lightly and traced a pattern in the leftover dressing on her plate.

Ophelia looked around at our faces. "It's funny how second children tend to be so much more easygoing than firsts," she said.

That pushed me over the edge. "Actually, Ophelia," I said, picking up a lemon wedge and squeezing it carefully into my Coke, "if you take a minute to count, you'll discover that Miranda is my father's *fifth* child. And Chandler is his fourth."

"Katherine," snapped my father, "that's enough."

Ophelia's mouth dropped open a little, and Douglas

kicked me hard under the table (which proved Ophelia didn't know what she was talking about, because Douglas is a second child, and he's one of the most uptight people I know).

We ate the last few bites of our food in silence. Ophelia gathered her photographs back into organized piles. Then my dad's beeper went off.

"Oh!" said Ophelia, obviously relieved. "That's Lynnea. I told her to page me when the kids were going to bed. I just want to call and say good night."

"I'll come with you." Dad started to get up, but Ophelia put a hand on his shoulder. "I can find the phone, Dale," she said. "Why don't you stay? You don't get too much time with these guys."

My father tipped his chair up so Ophelia could squeeze through. His eyes followed her across the restaurant to the pay phone. Her hair was down to her waist, I noticed. It shone in the lamplight. But she wasn't nearly as beautiful as my mother.

"How many days are you staying in Washington?" Douglas asked Dad.

Dad cleared his throat. "We fly out early Wednesday morning."

Douglas looked visibly disappointed.

"We'd hoped to stay longer," continued my father, looking at his empty coffee mug. "You know, see a little more of you kids. We'd like to do the Smithsonian, and Ophelia has more college friends she'd like to visit here . . . but the conference in Hawaii starts Friday morning. Chandler and Miranda will be jet-lagged. So, you know. We had to leave some time for settling in."

He cleared his throat again. When Douglas kept staring at him, he muttered, "We figured you couldn't . . ."

"What?" asked Douglas eagerly.

"Well, we planned on doing a little sight-seeing tomorrow. We figured your mother wouldn't want you missing school. But . . . if you wanted to and she'd let you, I guess you could come along."

"All of us?"

"Uh . . . sure." My dad squirmed, looking over his shoulder for Ophelia. "We'd love to take the three of you—if it's okay with your mother."

I bit my lip, avoiding Douglas's eyes, because I knew he was dying.

"There's *four* of us," I said slowly. "Could Alisa come too?"

My Dad didn't answer. I looked up at him, and he met my eyes across the table with a half-disgusted, half-embarrassed expression.

"Well?" I asked.

"Come on, Katherine." He was looking more and more uncomfortable. "Give me a break, here."

"What? I'm just asking, can she come too?"

"No," said my father. "She can't. Alisa is not my daughter—as you *very* well know."

"Well, why does that mean she can't come to the museum? She'll feel totally left out if we all go and she can't."

My dad sighed and looked away. Staring in the direction of the bar, he rolled a coffee stirrer between his fingers, and I realized he was craving a cigarette. So was I.

"It would make Ophelia uncomfortable," he said, finally looking back at me.

What a liar. It would make *him* uncomfortable.

"Mom won't let us go anyway," I said, shrugging. "It's a school day."

My father looked incredibly relieved.

"I have a math test," said Tracey.

Douglas didn't say anything. I couldn't look at him.

Ophelia headed back to the table, and my dad started digging in his wallet for his credit card.

Chapter Four

After school the next day, at three-thirty-five in the afternoon, we had our first official "family meeting" in the tree house. I made a huge bowl of buttered popcorn for the occasion—partly because I wanted it, and partly as a bribe to get Tracey and Douglas up there. I wasn't sure how they were going to react to the idea of a family meeting, since we'd never been a family meeting kind of family.

When the popcorn was ready, I found them in front of the TV, where they'd crashed as soon as they came in from the bus. Their backpacks, coats, and papers were strewn all over the floor. "Hey," I said, smiling as brightly as I could, "let's go outside and eat in the tree house." I rattled the popcorn in the bowl. "I need to talk to you guys about something important."

Douglas immediately dropped the remote control, rolled off the sofa, and came over to me. It's pathetic how easy he is to control with food. I think he might have a tapeworm or something. I told him that once, but he never did anything about it.

Tracey was harder. Turning reluctantly away from the television, she narrowed her eyes in a way that I particularly hate—like she's Sherlock Holmes or something, about to pronounce someone guilty of a crime. "I already ate," she said, glancing at the popcorn noncommittally. "Brian's sister had brownies on the bus—left over from cheerleading tryouts."

"Oh," I said, keeping the smile on my face with some difficulty. "Well, you don't have to eat. I've been thinking of a lot of stuff we need to talk about, though. Come on—Alisa gets home at four. We should hurry."

I spun around and headed for the yard. Fake smiles can only be maintained for so long, and I knew by then that they would both follow me—Douglas because of the popcorn and Tracey because she wouldn't want to be left out of whatever we were discussing. Tracey's hatred of exclusion is as predictable as Douglas's addiction to food.

We climbed the tree-ladder one by one—first Douglas, then me, then Tracey. There's barely room in the tree house to stand up, because my dad built it for us way back before he turned into a dirt-eating worm and left, when we were all under four feet tall. If you sit down, though, it can hold three grown-up people comfortably, and it's a great place to hang out. The walls, floor, and ceiling are made of grayish brown wood planks nailed together so tight, they keep out the rain, and screen windows open on four sides, with wooden storm flaps on pulleys. One whole wall is lined with red milk crates to hold notebooks and pencils and stuff. Back when we were little, the floor was cluttered with toys, but it isn't anymore (except that Snoopy playhouse-thing because it's too big and grimy to haul down the ladder). Alisa doesn't leave her stuff up there. As a matter of fact, she refuses to play in the tree house at all; she's afraid one day it might come crashing down out of the tree.

When I heard her explain that once, I thought it was very ironic because Alisa weighs about as much as a family-sized bottle of shampoo. If anyone should be worried about the tree house collapsing under them, it's me, because I'm the only one in my family who's overweight. According to an article I read in *Mother's Magazine,* I am exactly six to sixteen pounds over my target weight, depending on whether I have small, medium, or large bones. I have no way of knowing how bad my problem really is, because they didn't say how you were supposed to determine your bone size. (I guess if I really wanted to find out, I would have to get an X ray and then compare it to a lot of other X rays to see how big the average skeleton is, but I don't have the time or resources.)

Tracey, on the other hand, is beautiful. She has no freckles and no fat problems. As long as I can remember, she's always looked like a doll—first a Shirley Temple doll, and then a Malibu Barbie doll (except minus the boobs and with curlier hair). Douglas is freckly and redheaded like me and Alisa, but he is three inches taller than me and thin as a post. He wears ratty clothes and he has one pierced ear, which is supposed to look tough but unfortunately looks kind of silly. I suppose he *might* weigh more than me because guys are supposed to be heavier, but he doesn't have any muscles that I can see. Anyway, I've never asked him his weight because when it comes right down to it, if I am heavier than my brother who's less than a year younger than me, I don't want to know. It's bad enough having Barbie for a sister when you look like the Great Pumpkin yourself.

"Well," said Douglas through a mouthful of popcorn, "if this is about the sink, I've been thinking. When Mom gets up, we can call a plumber. But I think I can plug it up in the meantime so we can turn the main valve back on till then. It'll probably only be a few days."

"Douglas," I said, taking a deep breath, "it's not about the pipes."

"Well, if it's about Dad—"

"It's not about Dad either. I just . . . I think we should really *talk* about how we're running things. The situation with the house and food and Alisa—especially money and food." That didn't come out nearly as businesslike as I'd planned, which pissed me off, so I sat up straighter and added, "What I'm talking about are goals. Establishing the means and ends to a plan of *survival*." I looked at their faces to see if they understood what I was getting at.

Douglas obviously didn't, but he was happy to drink his Coke and wait for me to explain. Tracey had eaten exactly one small handful of popcorn, piece by piece, and was reaching for the cigarettes, looking suspiciously at the notebook on my lap. She didn't say a word.

Conversations like this make me tired, like I'm the only one in the world who speaks English. I dug my fingertips into the knees of my jeans. "Well?" I said finally.

"Well, what?" asked Douglas.

"What do you *think*?"

"What do we think of what?"

My mouth dropped open. If Douglas of all people didn't understand the seriousness of the situation we were in, it was hopeless. I was just about to surrender to personal rage and give up when Tracey leaned over, tapped out her half-smoked cigarette, and said in a low voice, "She means about *Mom,* Douglas. What are we going to do about Mom?"

I shut my mouth, shocked. Tracey never discussed our mom. She only talked about things like parties and boys and how annoying she thought it was that St. Agnes didn't have middle-school cheerleading. If conversations between Douglas and me ever got serious, she'd usually walk out of the room and call a friend or something.

Before I could recover my powers of speech, she kept going. "We're running out of food. The house is a sty. You're the only one who works, Douglas, and you don't make that much from a paper route once a week. I mean, for cigarette money, fine, but not groceries. Mommy's not getting up again in a few *days.* She's probably never gonna get up, she's probably going to *die* up there, and what Katherine means is, what the hell are we going to do?" Her nose suddenly got all red, and she clenched her jaws together. For one horrible minute I thought she was going to start crying, but she didn't—she just swallowed twice, grabbed her cigarette out of the ashtray, and lit it again before adding, "If you'd pull your face out of the popcorn bowl for two seconds, you might catch on, Douglas. You're supposed to be the genius."

Douglas gave a kind of half shrug and slouched down against the wall, folding his arms across his chest. Douglas really hates to get into an argument; he's not good at it. After a minute he wiped his hands on his knees to get rid of the popcorn crumbs and lit a cigarette for himself.

I actually wonder sometimes if Douglas might be totally missing the gene for aggression. I'm not sure that's possible, but I think someone should do an experiment about it. If they did, I would sign Douglas up to be a subject. He plays electric guitar, mostly heavy metal songs, but he only bothers to learn the sad, mellow parts. "Stairway to Heaven" is his favorite, for instance, but when he gets to the screaming, repetitive part, he loses interest and switches to the beginning of a different quieter song, like "Dust in the Wind." If Tracey and I get in a fight that lasts more than five minutes, he disappears to go for a walk or something because he can't stand it. He doesn't even like competitive sports, and I don't think he has many friends at school. He's too nervous to be popular. But when he's alone, he's cool. It's all a confidence problem. In a strange way I can relate to Douglas—even though I'm extremely competitive.

I looked down at my notebook and wondered what to say next so the conversation wouldn't turn into a fight. "I made a list of ideas—"

"You're not going to try to get the sherry away from her again, are you?" Douglas interrupted. "That was a nightmare. And anyway, it didn't work. Remember? I really think that would be stupid to try again."

I cleared my throat. "Calm down, Douglas. That's not what I mean. I don't think we can do anything about *Mom.* As long as she keeps eating, at least a little bit, she's not going to die. People don't die from being alcoholic, except after a long time like twenty years." I wasn't sure that was exactly true, but it made me feel better to say it.

"I mean, we need a plan for what to do about *us*—and Alisa. Especially Alisa. Because I think she's really upset—more than she shows. She's getting totally neglected. We need to figure out a way to keep things normal while Mom's in bed. So Alisa doesn't get emotionally scarred or something. Like we should eat together and have clean laundry, and make sure Alisa's getting enough nutrition. You know?" I was starting to feel better just talking about it. Making a list *always* helps. Having a plan.

"Maybe Tracey and I can get jobs to earn money," I continued. "And we should take turns reading to Alisa at bedtime. I read this article in *Mother's Magazine* that said reading is all-important for eight-year-olds. It helps their sense of security and their language skills. Plus, we should make these meetings a tradition, every day after school, I think. And also," I finished, taking a deep breath, "we should stop fighting with each other—at least in front of Alisa. It's probably sabotaging her sense of security."

I stopped to accept the cigarette Tracey was offering me. I lit it, and for a while no one said anything. We all just leaned back against three corners of the tree house, smoking. I watched their faces, trying to see how my ideas were going over. I was especially staring at Tracey. I didn't feel so much older than her like I always used to. We all have the same grayish green eyes, Tracey and Douglas and me. And I noticed we all looked kind of tough when we weren't smiling. That was good.

"Maybe we should just call Dad," suggested Douglas.

"We can't," said Tracey immediately in that same low voice.

"Why not?" Douglas argued, pulling at the lopsided neck of his tie. "Just because *you* guys hate him . . ."

"For one thing, they're going to be in Hawaii for a month, remember?"

"They gave us the phone number at the hotel."

"It doesn't matter," said Tracey. "We can't call him. If Dad found out Mom's been drunk for this long, he'd make us go stay with him and Ophelia in Michigan—and then what would happen to Alisa?"

With a shock of horror, I realized she was right. I'd never thought about that.

Douglas hesitated. "Well, maybe . . . if that happened, Alisa could come with us."

"Yeah, right." Tracey shook her head. "Are you blind? He wouldn't even take her to the museum."

Douglas didn't answer. I got a chill up my spine. She had a very good point.

The fact that Alisa had no family but us was something I'd always taken for granted. She was born two years after Dad disappeared with Ophelia, and all I know about her background is that she came from "a short affair." I have no idea *which* short affair, because like I already told you, my mom had a million boyfriends. As we all sat there, smoking and thinking, that fact suddenly seemed sort of strange to me. No one else I knew had some siblings from one father and another from somewhere else—somebody else, some mystery man. It was kind of unusual.

Strictly speaking, I guess Alisa was only our half sister. But she'd always seemed *more* related, not less. We all remembered the day she'd come home from the hospital, looking like a shriveled-up raisin in a yellow blanket. We'd been in love with her from that day on, carrying her around the house like she was made of spun glass. After Alisa was ten months old, my mom went back to work and we took over—sticking to Alisa like glue at the day-care lady's house, keeping all the other kids at arm's length. They were curious; they wanted to touch the baby too, but if any kid came too close, Tracey or Douglas or I would pinch him as hard as we could. "She's *ours,*" we'd say fiercely. "Get away."

By the time she was old enough for day care, we'd already taught Alisa to stand up by holding onto the coffee table, clap her hands, and say "bye-bye" and "Big Bird." In the years after that, we taught her to read *Green Eggs and Ham,* plant tomatoes, turn cartwheels, dial 911, tie her shoes, and everything else we could think of. Tracey even taught her to put on mascara. Alisa was special. She had no one but us. She belonged to us.

"Okay, you're right," said Douglas, interrupting my thoughts. "We can't tell Dad."

"We can't tell any teachers either," said Tracey. "They'll report Mom to Social Services and we'll get stuck in an orphanage."

Now Tracey was sounding a little more like her stupid self, and for some reason I found that comforting. "There are no such things as *orphanages* anymore," I said, even though I'd never intended to tell any teachers in the first place.

"Then foster homes."

"That's ridiculous."

But Douglas agreed with Tracey. "It's true," he said, "they might. We don't have any relatives who'd take us—except Aunt Laura. And she's *really* unbalanced." Aunt Laura was my mother's pothead sister in California. We'd only met her once.

"I *mean,*" I said, "it's ridiculous that they'd take us away from Mom. They couldn't do that."

Douglas shook his head. "They could, actually. That's what happened to Jamal and Theresa."

Jamal Washington had been Douglas's only good friend at St. Luke's, until one day he'd disappeared over summer vacation without even saying goodbye. He and his sister had been scholarship students, and as smart as Douglas. Smarter, even, according to Douglas.

"Jamal and Theresa were poor," I said. "Plus, they were abused. Remember? You told me that."

"Teachers have to tell the Department of Social Services if

they suspect any abuse or neglect at all. There's a law. If they don't, they get sued," said Tracey.

I stared at her. She was acting like a completely different person today. I wondered if she could have read that in a book.

"Theresa told me," she added, solving the mystery.

"Well, we're not abused," I said, exasperated.

"Neglected, abused," said Douglas, "it's the same thing. If DSS finds out how Mom is acting, they'll say she's neglecting us and take us away. And they'll put Mom in detox or a mental institution. They *will*," he said, cutting me off. "It happens all the time, Katherine." He didn't look stubborn, just matter-of-fact, like he was talking about science or something.

My stomach kind of twisted then, and we were all quiet for a long time. I imagined Alisa being dragged off alone, and my mother waking to an empty house . . . or locked up in a faraway hospital with white walls. I shuddered.

"If Social Services ever found out," I said, "we could run away to the woods and hide with Alisa. We could do that before we let them take us. We'd just hide in the woods and live there till they stop looking for us and then . . . go find Mom. And get her out of the hospital, or wherever. It wouldn't be that hard." I hated the outdoors, personally, and I knew I was sounding ridiculous, but I needed to say something to break the silence.

"And anyway," I added after a minute, looking Douglas straight in the eyes, and then Tracey, "it probably won't come to that."

They looked unblinkingly back at me. They trusted me, I could tell, and I suddenly felt extremely old. "If we're smart about how we act right now," I said, "it won't come to that.

We still have a chance to keep everything normal. If we just handle things right, then nothing bad will happen."

I believed myself when I said that. I believed we could handle anything, even if my mom never got back up—and sooner or later she *had* to. If Douglas, Tracey, and I tried hard enough, I thought we could keep everybody safe. Which just goes to show how stupid you can be when you're fifteen. Even if you're smart.

Chapter Five

In the end we came to ten conclusions before Alisa's school bus dropped her off and we had to break up the meeting. I wrote them all down in my notebook:

1. *Tree house meetings will now be daily at 3:30 p.m.*
2. *We will all start paying more attention to Alisa.*
3. *As of today, October 24th, we will not fight anymore.*
4. *Tracey will see how much food we have left, and make a menu so it will last as long as possible.*
5. *Katherine will maybe look into getting a job.*
6. *Don't waste any money. Only necessities.*
7. *Douglas will be treasurer.*
8. *Current assets: $33.25*
   After cigarettes are bought for tree house: $30.00
9. *Don't tell ANYONE about Mom. No friends, teachers, neighbors, relatives, grown-ups, anyone*

who looks like they're involved with the government.

10. *Don't act suspicious in any way.*
11. *Meet again tomorrow at this time.*

I guess I should explain about my personal notebooks. In case you haven't noticed already, I am an extremely organized person, and I like to write everything down. Because of that, ever since elementary school I have kept track of things in notebooks. I have two of them—they're both different but important.

The first one has a red cover and is very thick—probably three hundred pages, front to back. It's full of lists of things to do. Every list I've ever made is there; I've never thrown out a list. You never know when you might end up trying to make a plan in the future and needing to look at the stuff you were supposed to get done in the past. I tried to explain that to Douglas once but he said I was obsessive-compulsive. I told him I didn't care what he thought. Keeping lists is a good idea, and that has been proven over and over again in my life.

My other notebook is a list too. Not a list of things to do like my red notebook, but a list of things that are true about life. It has a nice dark green denim cover, which reminds me of a forest, and it's my oldest notebook—I started it in fourth grade. It fills up more slowly than the other one, but already it's about two-thirds full. Each page is completely covered with facts—things I have learned. A lot of them I've learned the hard way, and I wrote them down so I wouldn't have to learn them over again. Some are just trivia facts, but I figure you never know when you might need to refer to them.

After our meeting I opened this notebook and wrote facts #208–210. Just to give you an idea how the green notebook works, here's the whole page, as it looked that afternoon when I was finished:

Fact #204: Identical uniforms do not make everyone look alike. They make pretty people look prettier. They make ugly people look uglier.
(Source: Myself)

Fact #205: Left-handed and ambidextrous people have been shown in a study to be more creative than right-handed people.
(Source: Mother's Magazine*)*

Fact #206: No matter how much you ask God for something to happen or someone to get better, it will not work. Praying is most likely just a plot thought up by religious leaders to keep everyone busy.
(Source: Myself)

Fact #207: You can use paper towels in the coffee machine when you run out of filters and it works the same.
(Source: Douglas)

Fact #208: Under extreme pressure, stupid people become smarter. Evidence: Because of the Mom crisis, Tracey managed to put aside her shallow interests and give good suggestions in order to survive. Also look at the wars—you never hear about stupid people storming the Bastille or fleeing from the Nazis. This is probably due to the same stupid-smart principle.
(Source: Myself)

Fact #209: Teachers cannot be trusted to solve the problems of minors. They are obligated by law to tell the Department of Social Services if they even suspect child abuse, and then the government can take the kids away.

(Source: Theresa and Jamal Washington)

Fact #210: Drinking too much and not feeding your kids counts as child abuse.

(Source: Douglas)

There have been a few facts in the history of my green notebook that have turned out to be wrong. For instance, when I was in fifth grade, someone once told me you could cut a live earthworm in half and both halves would regenerate into new worms. I wrote this down immediately and told Douglas. He came back to me three days later and said he'd tried it on four specimens, but instead of producing eight live worms, he'd just ended up with four dead ones. He was very upset; he said his worms suffered to death all because of me and my faulty facts.

I knew that wasn't exactly true because as soon as Douglas had seen that the worms weren't regenerating, he'd have stomped on them to put them out of their misery. But still, I crossed that fact off the list. It was fact #24. In the five years since the worm incident, I'd accumulated over 180 facts—even allowing for the crossed out mistakes. Over those five years, even Douglas had come to respect the wisdom of my notebooks.

I'd packed up my writing things and was still in the tree house, spying out the window, when Alisa's school bus pulled up and she jumped out. I'd hoped she would look more cheerful than she had the day before; she was usually pretty energetic when she got home from school. Instead she looked worse. Even from so far away I could see how pale she was, and she hesitated on the sidewalk as her bus drove away—almost like she didn't know where to go, even though the house was right in front of her. She looked down at her blue sneakers and twisted one outward like a ballet dancer. Then she suddenly squatted down and picked something up off the sidewalk. I was too far away to see what it was.

Sighing, I pulled the tree house windows shut and climbed down the ladder. Tracey and Douglas had gone inside as soon as we ended our meeting—Tracey running because the phone was ringing. (Nineteen out of twenty calls that came to our house were for Tracey.)

I crossed the lawn to where Alisa was and crouched down beside her on the pavement. The thing she had in her hand was a crab apple, and she was using it to draw a picture on the sidewalk. I used to do that when I was little too.

"What are you drawing?" I asked her.

She looked up and smiled briefly, proving that she'd already forgiven me for snapping at her the day before. She never holds a grudge. "I'm drawing a lion," she said thoughtfully. "He's standing under a lamppost where the door to Narnia is."

I picked up a crab apple and began to twist the stem, automatically counting the number of twists until its head popped off. "The lion is from Narnia?"

"He's the king of Narnia," she said solemnly. "He's Aslan. He's king of the animals and children in all the worlds . . . like God."

Hopefully more reliable than God, I thought, but I didn't say it out loud.

"Hey," I said instead, "you want to go to the library today? I've got time to walk over with you." I smiled as I asked her, but she didn't look up, which confused me. I'd expected her to be thrilled; she was always begging me to take her to the library. She didn't say anything either; she just kept squashing her crab apple into the pavement—making bushy fur around the lion's face and neck. "Alisa?" I said again. Maybe she hadn't heard me. "You want to go with me to the library?"

She looked up suddenly. She seemed confused, like she'd just woken from sleep. "I got a note today from school," she said abruptly. "It's for Mommy." Before I could answer, she added, "I think it's bad. Maybe you should read it. Maybe we shouldn't go to the library."

My knees were starting to ache from squatting, so I gave up and sat all the way down on the sidewalk. Apparently we weren't going anywhere anyway. "A note from your teacher?" I asked her. I had a really hard time imagining Alisa misbehaving enough to warrant a note.

Alisa nodded. She pulled a sealed envelope out of her front jeans pocket and handed it to me. Suddenly I felt nervous, like I was the one in trouble. *Maybe her teacher noticed her clothes,* I thought. I didn't want to open it. What if Alisa's school had somehow already found us out, and this note was to say that Social Services were on their way over to take us away?

But that was ridiculous. As I tore the envelope open, Alisa stiffened. I wanted to reassure her but I didn't know how, so I just read the note fast to get it over with.

It was on flowered stationery. The top had the teacher's name in calligraphy: *Miss Edith Beatrice Barnes.*

Dear Mrs. Graham,

I would like to conference with you immediately regarding your daughter Alisa's progress. I have asked Dr. Pickel, the school psychologist, to be present as well. His schedule can accommodate a morning meeting on either Tuesday or Friday. Please respond at your earliest convenience.

Sincerely,
Edith Barnes

The first thing I thought was that if my mother *had* been awake to read the note, it would have pissed her right off. Her pet peeve was when a teacher or coach or the pediatrician expected her to drop everything for the sake of one of us. "Oh, that's just great," she used to say. "I'll just zoom right over as soon as my nails dry and my soap opera is finished. Good Lord, doesn't it ever occur to these people I have a life? Where do they think I get the money to pay them—off a tree?"

Alisa's fingers were digging into the knees of her jeans. Her nails were turning white. "Is she mad?" she asked.

I looked at her, wanting to hug her but at the same time feeling a weird sense of responsibility, like I should try to be at least sort of parental. "Why *would* she be mad?" I asked carefully.

Alisa looked at the letter in my hands. "Well . . . what did she *say*?" she countered.

Smart. I didn't smile, though. "Why would she be mad, Alisa?"

She paused and then crumbled. "She doesn't believe me."

"What doesn't she believe you about?"

"Narnia." Her voice was disappearing, so I reached out and took one of her hands to reassure her. Then it registered what she'd said: "Narnia." *Narnia?* Was this about that letter? "What . . . ," I started, then stopped. I couldn't figure out what question to ask. "What are you talking about?"

That came out wrong. Alisa bit her lip but kept her head up. "I told her I saw the door to Narnia," she said, her blue eyes looking not quite at me but off to one side. "And I *did.* In the woods. I was trying to get to it, but Miss Barnes came and caught me before I could. She ran faster than me. And she yelled at me and the door disappeared . . . because she made too much noise. She scared it away."

"The door to Narnia," I echoed stupidly, not understanding.

"I saw it. She didn't believe me. She thought I was running away from school. There's nothing past the fence anyway except woods. If I was going to run away, why would I run there? I told her that and she got mad." She met my eyes then. The memory seemed to make her indignant.

"You were past the fence?" I dropped Alisa's hand and sat back. The playground at the elementary school is completely enclosed by a tall wire fence, and everyone knows you're not allowed past it. That rule is the first thing you learn when you start kindergarten. Behind the fence is a wooded lot—part of the grounds of a private halfway house for rich juvenile delinquents. The woods are thought to be peopled with escaped perverts and drug dealers. I remembered from my own elementary school days how insane the teachers got if anyone ever went *near* that fence, let alone climbed it. "What were you doing past the fence? You climbed the *fence*?" That fence was five feet high, at least. Third-graders never went anywhere near it. They usually stayed right by the school, playing hopscotch and jacks.

"To get to the door," she said.

"The door to Narnia."

"Yes." She was looking at me like *I* was the third-grader and *she* was in high school.

"You were playing that the door to Narnia was past the fence? And you tried to climb over the fence, and Miss Barnes—"

"Not *playing*," Alisa corrected. "It was real. I was looking at the woods, and I saw this curvy branch that made an arch like a doorway. And then I looked *through* it and I could see the lamppost in the snow back there, so I knew it was the door into Narnia. I wanted to get to Aslan, but Miss Barnes ruined it. She pulled me off the fence and the door disappeared. And then she didn't believe me that it was even there." She brooded. "She kept me after school while she wrote that note. I almost missed the bus. What did she write?"

I was totally at a loss for what to say. I wanted to know exactly what Alisa had said to the teacher, word for word. I hoped she hadn't sounded as insane as she did right then. But when I remembered that the note had requested a meeting with a psychologist, I guessed I had my answer already.

"She didn't say anything bad," I said. "She just wants to meet with Mom."

Alisa panicked. "But Mommy can't go there—"

"It's okay. We'll just write her a note and pretend it's from Mom. We'll say she has a cold and can't come in this week, that's all."

Alisa thought about that. She still looked worried. "I didn't mean to make her angry. She got so mad."

I sighed. There was no way I was going to talk about Mom being an alcoholic or C. S. Lewis being dead right then—not when Alisa was already so upset. We'd have to do it some other time. I wondered what she'd seen behind the fence. Was it just an optical illusion? Was she going crazy? I wondered if it was possible for children to have hallucinations because of stress and bad nutrition. Then I remembered an article I once read about childhood schizophrenia, and I shuddered.

I wanted some more time to think, but my brain felt all

thought out. I knew I should go in and start my homework—I was a day behind already. Plus, now I'd have to forge the note from my mom to Alisa's teacher. . . . *Ugh.* My head hurt again, and I reached out and took Alisa's hand.

"Look," I said sort of sternly, "no matter what you think you see, you can't ever climb that fence again. You understand? It's dangerous."

She stared at me, surprised. "Are *you* mad?" she demanded. She was turning even whiter. Obviously this was a disaster she hadn't even thought of.

I stood and pulled her to her feet. "No, I'm not mad. But stay away from the fence. You want to come inside and have popcorn? I made a lot."

She picked up her backpack from the sidewalk and wordlessly followed me to the house, watching my face carefully.

"I'm not mad," I said again.

"Your mouth is clenched."

She was too smart to be eight. That was probably half her problem. "I'm just a little stressed out," I told her. "Worried, but not mad."

At that, she seemed to relax. She hugged me around the waist with her stringy arm. "You don't have to be worried," she said. "As soon as I talk to Aslan, I'll come back. I won't leave you here alone."

Chapter Six

She's probably going crazy, I thought. *What if she's really losing it? Maybe she* does *need a child psychologist.*

It was 2:15 the next day, according to the school clock, and I was sitting in my least favorite class, Religion and the Early Church. As I said before, I'm an extremely good student (even in religion, which I hate). But that day I couldn't concentrate at all, probably because it was eighth period and I'd only slept five hours the night before. I was too sleepy to take notes, so my mind kept drifting back to that conversation with Alisa. Also, I was suffering from what were probably the initial stages of malnutrition, thanks to Tracey's new menu.

Douglas, Alisa, and I had found it taped to the refrigerator door that morning, a detailed graph-paper chart labeled OFFICIAL MENU FROM NOW ON. Under the column marked WEDNESDAY, OCTOBER 25TH, Tracey had penciled in only half a doughnut and three gulps of Hi-C for each of us in the breakfast slot, with a thirty-five-cent allowance for lunch. Thirty-five cents wouldn't even buy a hot dog at the cafeteria, and Tracey knew it. I asked her, didn't she think that was a little *extreme*? But she said if we stuck to her menu exactly, we could survive a full month of school days on the money we had, and use all the groceries we'd save to last equally as long at home.

When she put it that way, it seemed at least worth trying—a month sounded like a long time. But when it came right down to it, I wasn't so sure it was going to work. At the lunch counter that day, I'd realized thirty-five cents gave me a choice between two items: milk, or a small bag of Fritos. After thinking it over, I chose the Fritos, which turned out to be a mistake. They were way too salty to eat with no drink, and I proceeded to spend the entire two hours after lunch gradually shriveling into a dehydrated state so severe that by the time I got to religion class, my tongue felt like it was made of flannel.

As I sat there in class, chewing on my pencil, I wondered if my hydration level might be in the process of becoming a medical emergency. I wondered where Tracey, Douglas, and Alisa were at that moment, and whether *they'd* chosen the Fritos, and whether they were experiencing the same problem. *Alisa can't live this way,* I thought. *She's still growing. And Douglas is probably passed out in a hallway somewhere.*

Meanwhile Mr. Dodgson, the religion teacher, paced back and forth at the front of the room, scuffing the carpet with his shiny new shoes and lecturing on and on about something related to the early Church—I'd lost track of what, exactly. "Blah-blah-blah," he droned, "blah-blah-blah . . . which leads us to the apostle Paul, who's just experienced *what* cathartic and spectacular event?"

We should have given Alisa *some extra money, at least. What if her teacher noticed she only had thirty-five cents?*

"On the road to Damascus?" Mr. Dodgson prompted,

scanning the rows of desks for a raised hand. "Who remembers?"

Still nobody answered. I looked at the clock. There were fifteen more minutes till the last bell. The second hand spiraled around and around, and nobody said a word. It went reluctantly right side up, then upside down. Right side up, long pause, upside down. Insanely slowly, like it was rotating through cooked taffy instead of just air.

Anyway, I thought, *even if she is crazy, we can't afford a child psychologist. And maybe she's not. Probably she's just* imaginative *and those jerks at the elementary school have some kind of persecution complex.*

"Come on," persisted Mr. Dodgson, turning a little red, "I know you all know this from your reading. What's just happened to Paul?"

I put my pencil down, irritated. *He got converted. Duh.*

I wondered whether, if I continued to watch the clock, I'd lose my mind. I'd read an article once where someone went insane from watching the second hand on a clock—an Iranian hostage trapped in a cell with nothing else to look at. He'd been malnourished and dehydrated too. Reluctantly I steered my gaze from the second hand to Mr. Dodgson, who was standing up at the front of the room, practically on tiptoe, desperately trying to catch someone's eye.

"Da-*mas*-cus," he said again, as though speaking to the hearing impaired. "Sara? Brittany? Louise?" He'd taken off his wire-framed glasses and was holding them in his chubby hand as his anxious brown eyes searched one row of faces, then another, practically begging for any movement or sign of understanding.

My stomach gurgled. I wished somebody would just answer the question, because *I* couldn't without violating my strict rule never to voluntarily talk out loud in class. (I put that rule into effect halfway through seventh grade, when I started to get a reputation as a brain. Fact #105 in my green notebook: *People persecute brains. Reason—unknown. Even teachers don't like it when you're too smart. Probably feel threatened. (Source: Myself).*

Mr. Dodgson had probably been a brain when he was young. He was at least thirty-five or forty, I figured, and I'd heard someone say that he was *still* in school—at Georgetown University, working on his Ph.D. Mr. Dodgson was new to St. Agnes that year, and it was obvious from the very first day of class that he'd never taught high school before. Most teachers are dull, but he was painful. All he ever talked about was the Bible, which seemed to make him all happy and excited for reasons I could not possibly fathom. It made the rest of us mad—not only because it was infernally boring, but because in tenth grade, we were supposed to have had this other teacher, Ms. Bledsoe, who talked about interesting things in her religion class, like women's rights and psychology. We'd all been looking forward to her class for years. But then, over summer vacation, she announced she was pregnant and quit, so we were stuck with Mr. Dodgson.

Actually, according to Sara Whittaker, whose mother was on the board, there was a lot more to the Ms. Bledsoe story. "You know why she had to quit?" Sara had asked us all on the first day of class. (For some reason Mr. Dodgson wasn't there yet—he must have been getting our textbooks or something.)

We all *thought* we knew the reason: Ms. Bledsoe was one of those skinny ladies who look like they swallowed a basketball even when they're only a few months along, so it had been obvious the previous spring that she was pregnant. We figured she'd quit to stay home with the baby.

"No," Sara told us. "Ms. Bledsoe wanted to teach this year anyway. The school board *made* her resign."

"Why?"

"Because she wasn't married. Her boyfriend got her pregnant."

We were all quiet.

"So?" someone had finally asked.

"So," said Sara meaningfully, raising her eyebrows, "it looked bad. For a *religion* teacher to be single and pregnant? The school board was afraid of a scandal, so they just made up some excuse to fire her."

"Isn't that illegal?"

"That's exactly what my mother said," Sara told us. "But those kinds of laws don't apply to private schools. It's all political. Alumni donations keep St. Agnes and St. Luke's running, and if anything like that makes the schools look bad, the alumni stop giving. That's just the way it works. Anyway, the school board is about eighty percent male, and my mother says they're totally sexist."

"Who'd they hire instead?"

"Some guy that went to school with Dean Schmidt. My mother says he's totally inexperienced—they just hired him at the last minute. He substituted at St. Luke's last year, but that's it. He's never even really *taught* before."

Right after Sara told us that story, Mr. Dodgson had entered the room and introduced himself for the first time. I remember feeling sorry for him because I knew he was doomed. No matter how good a teacher he was, we would all hate him. And then it turned out he was heinously boring anyway.

The only thing that occasionally made Mr. Dodgson mildly interesting was his tendency to get more flustered under pressure than any other human being I'd ever seen. The more nervous he got, the more he fidgeted and qualified. Right then he was starting to sweat because nobody would answer his question. "Marnie Adleman," he said, finally choosing the first name on his alphabetical class list, "can you tell us what happened to Pete—uh, Paul, please?"

I let my chin fall forward onto my hands. It was too bad for Mr. Dodgson that *Adleman* started with *A*. Marnie was the meanest girl in our whole class. The second most popular. (Sara Whittaker was the first, then Marnie, then Brittany and Louise Gill.)

The weird thing about Marnie was that there wasn't anything about her that *should* have made her popular. With the rest of them, you could sort of see how they got that way. Like, Sara Whittaker was kind of elegant, and soft-spoken, with a face like J.F.K.'s wife before she got old and died. Even besides her mother being on the board, you just looked at Sara and got the feeling she was born to be Queen. Brittany and Louise were pig-nosed twins—blond and insanely rich, with a myriad of horses and polo-playing relatives. They stuck to Sara's left and right without ever saying anything, so their personalities weren't exactly offensive. But Marnie was different. She wasn't rich *or* pretty—just wiry, obnoxious, and afraid of no one. She had a face like a weasel, and she'd climbed the social ladder by scaring everyone else out of the way—insulting them behind their backs or right to their faces. (Really pointed, specific, mean insults.) I suppose the only good thing about Marnie was that she was sort of funny, if you like mean humor, but I don't.

"I dunno, Mr. Dodgson," said Marnie coolly, bouncing one of her thin bare legs, which was crossed over the other. "I don't recall. What city did you say this happened in?"

"In *Damascus*," Mr. Dodgson repeated helpfully.

Marnie raised her eyebrows in a way that showed she thought Mr. Dodgson was an idiot. She yawned without covering her mouth. Then she spit out her retainer, put a piece of bubble gum in her mouth, and started chewing. "I just don't recall," she said through the gum.

At the next desk over, Sara Whittaker ran her fingers through her shiny nut-colored hair and raised her hand. "Mr. Dodgson," she said politely, "I don't mean to interrupt but I think the wall clock might be slow. My watch says it's two-thirty already."

Mr. Dodgson looked startled and squinted at the clock, but he couldn't see it because he'd taken his glasses off. He fumbled around trying to fit them back on his face, but his hands shook so the glasses clapped on his nose and bounced down to the floor. When he bent to pick them up, I could see the perfect circle of his bald head like a cantaloupe. Around the edges, brown tufty hair was combed sideways over the bald spot, and it occurred to me what he looked like: a medieval monk. If he hadn't been wearing a suit and tie, he'd have looked a lot like Friar Tuck.

"Well . . . Do you think?" he said, straightening up. "I don't know . . . Does anyone else have a wristwatch?"

We all had wristwatches. They all said 2:19. Not that it mattered, because no one who didn't have a death wish was going to contradict Sara Whittaker. Those of us in the nonpopular three-quarters of the class had learned that lesson way back in seventh grade—memorized it along with the school hymn and our locker combinations.

Mr. Dodgson shifted on his feet and glanced helplessly at his own wrists, neither of which wore a watch. "Well," he said, "let's just . . . finish quickly and then . . . Can anyone, uh, tell me about Paul?" He was beginning to look like a trapped animal, but I could tell he didn't want to back down. He probably believed he was proving something to us by sticking to his question.

Something about the way Mr. Dodgson was both stubborn and terrified at the same time reminded me of Douglas. It was like watching the pilot of a crashing plane, wild with fear but refusing to bail out. I sighed, then raised my hand.

"Yes!" He gestured wildly in my direction. "Yes . . . Kathy? Katherine?"

"Uh," I said slowly, "he had his conversion . . . I think." (When forced to answer questions, it's best at least not to seem confident.) "He saw a bright light and he decided he'd been wrong about things."

"Wrong about what?"

Oh come on, I thought, *do we have to prolong this?* Brittany gave me a snide sideways look, and I stared down at the graffiti on my desk.

"Wrong about *God,*" I said with finality so he wouldn't take advantage and keep making me talk.

Mr. Dodgson flushed with triumph. "Well, yes!" he said, smiling. "*Yes.* That's right. I guess we're finished. Don't forget the homework on First Corinthians, chapter—"

He never finished the sentence because the sound of eighteen notebooks slamming and the general stampede of people pushing into the hallway drowned him out completely.

I'd already zipped my backpack and was halfway to the door when I realized Mr. Dodgson was calling me. "Katherine? Katherine Graham?"

I considered making a break for it, but our new rule flashed in my head like a neon warning sign: *Don't act suspicious in any way.* I figured you couldn't get more suspicious than bolting from a classroom when a teacher was speaking to you, so I made myself stop, repress, and turn around.

"Yes, sir?" (It's a really galling rule at St. Agnes: you have to call every teacher *sir* or *ma'am,* which makes you feel like you're either in the air force or working at one of those cologne counters at Bloomingdale's.)

Mr. Dodgson motioned for me to come over, then began erasing the chalkboard with gusto, creating a poisonous-looking cloud of dust. I went and stood in front of his desk, impatiently watching his back while the chalky air floated into my nostrils and itched at the back of my throat.

I guessed he probably wanted to thank me for rescuing him in class. He didn't say anything at all, though, and after a minute or two I started to feel stupid, just standing there. I shifted my backpack to my right shoulder. Finally I cleared my throat loudly.

When he'd obliterated every trace of his lecture notes, Mr. Dodgson turned around, smiled at me, and squeezed himself into the old office chair behind his desk. Then he began to forage through his top desk drawer. I noticed he looked a lot less weak and helpless close up. He pulled out his attendance book and flipped through its pages deliberately. His eyes looked gentle and a little mad at the same time—the expression was familiar somehow, but I couldn't think why right away. Then all at once I stiffened. He looked like my dad. Before he left, back when he was nice.

"Is something wrong, Mr. Dodgson? I need to catch my bus." My voice came out high, hostile, and way too loud.

He put his attendance book down and paused. Then he leaned back in his chair and looked straight at me. "Katherine," he said—just that, like it was a sentence by itself. I wasn't sure what to make of it, but I could tell he wasn't flustered anymore, because his eyes rested on my face instead of darting around in search of an escape route, like when he was teaching. All that erasing must have calmed him down.

"You weren't in class Monday," he said.

"Oh. Right . . . I was sick Monday."

"I remember you said." He adjusted his glasses and asked kindly, "How are you feeling today?"

I frowned, trying to figure out if there was a trap somewhere in this. "I'm fine. Much better."

"Good." He smiled again. "I'm glad."

And your point? I jerked the sleeves of my blazer down over the cuffs of my blouse, trying not to let any irritation show in my face.

Mr. Dodgson looked down and grasped the edges of the attendance book. "I spoke with the administrative secretary yesterday . . . Mrs. Schmiedler, I believe it is. She mentioned she hadn't received a call or written excuse for your absence. Of course you know you're required to have one within forty-eight hours. Otherwise your absence is counted as . . . well, as *un*excused."

Finally I got it. He thought I'd skipped class. None of my other teachers had even bothered to check with the office because I had such a good reputation. Since Mr. Dodgson was brand-new, he was probably following the attendance procedure straight out of the book.

"Oh," I said, feeling a little relieved. "Well, my mother couldn't *call* in because she has laryngitis. In fact, she just had her tonsils out, so she can't talk at all. She gave me a note but . . . I forgot to bring it. I'll bring it tomorrow."

"Laryngitis?" His expression changed to one of concern.

"Yes, sir," I said, beginning to relax. I've always been good at lying. "Actually, our whole house is contagious—that's why I couldn't come on Monday. I thought I was coming down with it. But I guess not."

"Ah," said Mr. Dodgson. "I see."

"I really hate to miss school," I continued, stealing a subtle glance at my watch. "I've only been absent once before." It was 2:29. Still plenty of time to get to my locker and make the bus. If I hurried, I could probably get a seat in back with Tracey so we could talk about this moronic menu of hers.

But Mr. Dodgson wasn't moving. He wasn't packing up his things or anything. He was just looking at me.

I took a step sideways toward the door, checking my watch again as a hint, in case he'd forgotten about the school bus. *Okay, come on, let me out.* I took another step sideways as sort of a question mark.

"It must have been an awfully traumatic day for you," said Mr. Dodgson.

I stepped back, confused. "A . . . well, sort of, but . . ."

"Your sister told me you'd also badly cut your thumb. She mentioned stitches."

Oh. Shit. I'd forgotten Tracey had Mr. Dodgson for New Testament. *That blabbermouth idiot. She must have told him something different on Monday.*

"It must have been a terrible time in the emergency room, with potential laryngitis and a severed thumb as well. Was your mother with you, too?"

Shit shit shit shit . . .

"Or was she in another part of the hospital, having her tonsils operated on?" he concluded dryly.

I felt my mouth open slightly as I fumbled for an answer, but I couldn't think of anything to say. My mind felt like a stalled car. Finally I just shut my mouth and let my backpack slide down my arm to the ground. It hit the floor with a defeated clunk.

For a minute we were both quiet, while Mr. Dodgson

waited for me to either confess or keep lying. When I didn't do either, he helped me along. "Perhaps I should call your mother and see how she's feeling."

"No," I said through my teeth, struggling to stay polite but not quite managing the "sir." "I lied about Monday. I wasn't sick. Please don't call my mother; I'll just serve the detention." *I can't believe I felt sorry for you, you jerk. See if I ever rescue you again. I hope Sara and Marnie eat you alive.*

"Now." Again, it was a sentence, not a question.

"Yes, sir." *I hope you get high blood pressure and die.*

"All right, then—have a seat." Mr. Dodgson's smile wrinkles were in full force. I couldn't imagine why, unless he got some kind of weird thrill out of imprisoning students. Spinning around, I picked up my backpack, walked to the back of the room, and swung into a desk right below the clock with the crawling second hand.

Another two hours of this place. I'll be dead by four-thirty. I'm going to kill Tracey. Kill *her . . .*

"Can you get a ride home later?" Mr. Dodgson asked suddenly, as though the thought had just occurred to him.

"I'll take the sports and activities bus. It leaves at four-thirty."

"All right." He pulled a stack of papers out of his battered briefcase and began to look around for his green grading pen. "I'll sit here with you till then. Why don't you start on the homework?"

I was too angry to ask to go to the water fountain.

During the next two hours, which seemed like two years, Mr. Dodgson just quietly graded his papers and occasionally looked over at me, with that same gentle-mad-amused look. After the first five minutes, the bell rang to officially end classes. Twenty-five silent minutes after that, I pulled my green notebook out of my backpack and wrote,

Fact #211: People have got absolutely no idea how to lie right. When constructing a lie, always make everyone around you memorize it too, so they don't tell a different one, or the truth, and screw up your alibi.
(Source: The Mr. Dodgson incident of October 25th, Tenth Grade)

Fact #212: Stupid people such as Tracey should never be put in charge of things that affect other people's lives.
(Source: Dehydration incident, same day, see above)

By the time Mr. Dodgson finally let me out at four-fifteen, I was convinced my tongue had swollen to twice its natural size. To make matters worse, it was pouring rain outside, and I hadn't brought a raincoat or an umbrella to school with me. I hate rain.

As I was packing up my things to go, Mr. Dodgson leaned forward over his desk, trying to catch my eye. "Uh, Katherine," he said kindly, "you're one of my best students. I hope this doesn't affect how you feel about, er, class." He was obviously trying to make peace.

Yeah, right, I thought. *You stupid imbecile. My kidneys are failing because of you.* Not to mention I would probably get pneumonia from walking home from the bus in the rain.

"You know," he continued, "if there's a legitimate *reason* you can't come to class, you can tell me what it is. Maybe we could . . . can . . . well, it's better if I know the truth."

Ha. You will be the last *to know. I will be* dead *before you know.*

"Yes, sir," I said, keeping all expression out of my voice. "That's a good point. Can I please go now, though? The second bus is going to leave."

He sighed and leaned back in his chair, deflated. "Yes

. . . yes, of course you can go now," he said sadly. "Have a good after—well, evening."

I didn't answer, or even look up as I passed his desk. I just hoisted my backpack onto my shoulder and walked straight out the door to the water fountain. By the time I finally got a drink, I was so pissed at Tracey and Mr. Dodgson and St. Agnes in general, I'd forgotten I even had a mother to worry about.

Chapter Seven

It didn't take long to remember again.

It was almost five-thirty and starting to hail when the bus dropped me off. The sports bus only stops at the top of our street, five blocks from our house, so I had to walk the rest of the way home through the rain. The sky was dark, and the wind was blowing strong enough to bend the tops of the trees so everything looked like the scenery of a Halloween special on TV.

As I walked along the edge of the road, covering my head with a textbook and scuffing through wet piles of leaves at the edges of our neighbors' lawns, I started to get a crawly feeling in my stomach. My rage over the detention was starting to fade, and it occurred to me that I'd been gone almost ten hours—anything could have happened in that time. I wanted to see Alisa and make sure she was all right. I worried about the note Tracey and I forged to Miss Barnes, saying Mom had a cold. And I needed to see Douglas and Tracey—I wasn't sure why, even. I just needed to see them. I started to walk faster.

The rain brought the smells of suppers cooking out onto the street, and I glanced sideways at the neighbors' houses—crowded rows of kitchen windows all lit up on both sides of the road. For a minute I worried that people inside might be watching me, and wondering where my mother was. But that was stupid. It wasn't the kind of street where people knew each other, or cared. People were always moving in and out of the houses on the way to somewhere else. The only neighbors we'd ever known well enough to even call by name were some Iranian kids who used to live two houses down from us, and they'd long since moved back to the Middle East.

Still, I thought, people *might* wonder. I passed a white-brick house with a chain-link fence and three cats sitting on the porch, out of the rain. There were no lights on inside. I knew that an old lady lived by herself in there, because I always saw her walking around the neighborhood in the mornings. If she had nothing better to do, she might be spying on us. She might walk by our house every day and wonder why my mother's car never moved from the same spot in the driveway. She might notice that our leaves weren't raked neatly into piles like everyone else's . . . I hadn't thought of that, till just then. The crawly feeling got worse and worse, until finally I started running. I jogged the last two blocks to our house with my heart pounding so hard I could feel it pushing against my lungs.

When I got to the end of our driveway, I stopped. Our house looked different somehow, but my brain was tired from worrying and running, so the meaning of the differences didn't click right away. For a minute I just stood there in the rain, trying to catch my breath and staring at the house like you stare at someone who's just gotten their braces off and you can't quite figure out how they've changed. I looked at the familiar lawn, crab-apple tree, red bricks, and shutters until the first strange thing hit me: There were no lights on inside.

Right after that the second thing hit much harder, like a punch. The driveway was empty. My mother's car was gone.

I don't even remember what I did with my backpack. I think I threw it down on the sidewalk somewhere as I ran. I banged the front door open and, still hanging on to the inside door knob, yelled, "Mommy?"

No one answered. I threw my soggy textbook on a kitchen chair and went around flipping on all the lights. "Mom? Douglas? Tracey? Where are you guys? Where is everyone?" Hurrying through the foyer, living room, Tracey and Alisa's bedroom, I flipped on light after light and found nobody—no note, nothing.

My shoes slipped on the linoleum and hardwood floors, so I kicked them off and ran upstairs, missing the staircase light, but continuing in the gloom rather than bothering to turn around. One by one, I pushed open the doors off the hallway. Douglas's room, mine, both bathrooms—they were all empty. Then I hesitated for a second and kicked my mom's door open too, switching on the brass floor lamp just inside the door.

She wasn't there. The room looked exactly the same, stank the same of rotting food, bad breath, and sherry, but the unmade bed was empty and the quilts were in a clump, half on the bed and half on the floor.

I shut the door again and stood there, breathing hard and staring at the wall. Then I covered my eyes with my hands and slid down to a sitting position on the rug.

They were gone.

For a few seconds I couldn't make myself think at all. I

looked out through the cracks between my fingers and noticed weird details, like how rain-soaked my navy stockings were, even down where my shoes had covered the feet. There were damp footprints all over the carpet where I'd run. Strands of soaked hair had fallen down across my eyes and were curling into the reddish brown ringlets that my mom used to love when I was little. She used to tell me how lucky I was that my hair had natural wave. Hers was shiny and straight then. She didn't start perming it until after my father moved out.

They're gone, I thought. *The government must have come and taken them away.*

I remembered how my mother used to struggle to get all my hair in a ponytail before school, way back before Alisa was even born, when my parents were still married. She used to laugh a lot then. I always told her knock-knock jokes while she was helping me get ready.

Maybe she's dead. Why else would the government have come? How could they have known?

The clock on the hallway table started chiming six, and it occurred to me that wherever everyone was, dead or alive, the reason I wasn't with them was Mr. Dodgson. I would most likely never see my family again, and it was his fault.

I'm going to remember this day and hate him for the rest of my life, I thought. *When I grow up, when I get old. Always.*

All of a sudden I heard a noise downstairs—a thump, and then the familiar sound of the side door crashing open. I pulled my hands from my face and froze, sitting up straight against the wall. *The Social Services people,* I thought. *They came back.*

I looked around the hallway for somewhere to hide. Before I could decide on a place, the door downstairs creaked on its hinges and slammed shut. I heard someone walk hurriedly through the kitchen, and stood up as quietly as I could manage, edging toward the walk-in linen closet. Turning the knob softly, I was about to step inside when I heard another thump downstairs, and a shout.

"Katherine? Hey! Katherine, are you in here?"

It was Tracey.

Thank God, thank God, thank God. I turned and ran down the stairs as fast as I could go.

"Hey, Katherine—" she began.

I didn't even catch my breath before I started yelling. "What are you, an idiot? Where have you been? Are you some kind of moron?"

"Listen—"

"Do you know how scared I was, you jerk? You think you could maybe, I don't know, leave some kind of *note* or something so I don't have absolute *apoplexy* walking in here?"

"Katherine, shut up!" she said.

As mad as I was, I actually did stop shouting. There was something about Tracey's face that made me.

"We're out in the tree house," she said, pushing her hair out of her eyes. "You better get out there quick, because Mom's gone and Alisa's sick . . . and Douglas doesn't know what the hell he's doing."

The flood of relief I felt from seeing her was so strong, it was filling up my head like some warm, fizzy drink, and I had to fight very hard to listen to what she was saying. I repeated her words in my head until they made sense. Mom's gone, number one. Alisa's sick, number two. The government people aren't here, number three. Next step: Go to the tree house.

"Where's Mom?" I asked her, beginning to look around for my shoes.

"At the store, I think. I don't know—she talked to Douglas, not me. I'll tell you in the tree house. Just come *on*." She pulled on my arm.

I yanked it back. "Wait until I get my shoes at least. Jeez." After a quick search I found my shoes in the living room, pulled them on over my soggy stockings, and followed her back out into the rain.

We ran across the lawn toward the tree house, slipping on the icy wet grass. Both of us were still in our school clothes, which made the whole situation seem even stranger, like it was happening in a dream.

"Where the hell were *you* all afternoon?" Tracey shouted over the wind. Her voice lacked any real enthusiasm, so I could tell she was as relieved to see me as I was to see her.

I shook my head. "I'll tell you later."

Under the tree house we were out of the brunt of the rain, and as we climbed toward the trapdoor, yellow light poured down on us from up high. I felt like someone beaming up into a UFO or something. The light turned out to be coming from an antique oil lantern that Douglas had bought at a garage sale and smuggled up to the tree house a few months earlier. We'd never actually lit it before, and I was about to ask if they were sure it was safe, when my eyes focused on Alisa, who was behind the lantern, in Douglas's lap, hanging on to his tie like it was a rip cord, and throwing up all over his legs and the floor.

Douglas was kneeling awkwardly, and holding Alisa's hair back from her forehead. He was attempting to hold her face over a bucket so the vomit would land there instead of all over his school pants, but she kept squirming in his arms, so it didn't really work. After a few seconds she raised her head and nodded, and Douglas sat back, pulled her onto his lap, and rocked her while she sobbed in an awful hopeless wailing way that made me want to cry too. Judging from the state of Douglas's pants, this had been going on for a while.

I stared back and forth from Tracey to Douglas.

"We think she has the flu," said Tracey. "The teacher sent her home early."

I swallowed. "How early?"

"Before lunch."

"How could she? Who picked her up?" I tried to keep my voice calm, but I could feel it getting shrill in spite of myself. "It's freezing out here. How come you're out *here* if she's sick. Douglas, what is going *on*? Where's Mom?"

Douglas didn't answer. He just shot me a warning look and shook his head.

At the same time, Alisa twisted around in Douglas's lap to look at me. She'd just noticed I was there.

"Katherine?" she asked, hiccuping. "Katherine?" Then she stopped, looked away, moaned, and threw up again, missing the bucket entirely. After that she went into kind of a coughing fit, and started crying again.

"We should go back to the house now," said Tracey flatly. "You're right; it's freezing." I noticed for the first time that she was crying too. Her face was white and covered with tear streaks. I checked Douglas and saw that his was the same.

It was a dumb time for questions, obviously. "Yeah. Wait. Yeah. I'll climb down first, and you guys hand her to me, okay?"

They both nodded. They looked like a couple of concentration camp victims—like people who are so tired and miserable they don't care what happens anymore. Tracey waited till I was almost down the ladder, then leaned over the lamp to put the flame out, while Douglas lay down on his stomach by the trapdoor. He passed Alisa down, and I carried her like a rag doll in my arms all the way back to the house. It was almost like the old days, when we used to play house out in the backyard, only Alisa was too sweaty and hot and sick to be a doll, and the whole thing was too much like a nightmare to be a game.

It was a couple of hours later by the time I got any of my questions answered. Alisa had finally fallen asleep, after taking a bath and swallowing some children's Tylenol I'd found up in one of the medicine cabinets. Tracey was with her in their bedroom, doing her homework and keeping an eye on Alisa while she slept. Douglas and I sat in silence in the living room, wrapped up in army blankets because the house was freezing but nobody knew how to turn on the oil burner downstairs.

I couldn't stop thinking about Alisa. The whole time I'd been helping her in the tub, and getting her pajamas on, she'd been shivering and crying. She kept saying, "Mommy, where's Mommy?" over and over again, and I didn't know the answer.

"So," I said to Douglas finally. "Will you please tell me where Mom is?"

Douglas sighed and pushed his hair back from his face. I'd made coffee, and the steam from our mugs went up between us as we sat on either end of the sofa, facing each other. The clock on the nearby table ticked, and I braced myself for his answer. I figured she was probably dead, or he would have told me where she was by now.

"I don't know," he said softly. "She said she was going to the store, but that was, like . . . five hours ago. She said she was going to pick up a prescription for Alisa."

I pulled my blanket tighter around me. "You talked to her, then? She was awake? She could talk?"

He nodded. "Yeah, she could talk. I think she was getting better. You know? I mean, at least—" He stopped, then started again. "She was wobbly. She kept crying." He looked like he was going to add something, but then thought better of it and just said, "But yeah, she was . . . talking."

I was so relieved, I relaxed my hold on my mug, and some of the coffee spilled over onto the bunched-up blanket on my lap. "So Mom was *sober* when Alisa's teacher called? She went and got her at school?"

He nodded again. "I guess. When I got home, Mom and Alisa had just come from the pediatrician's office. Alisa wasn't as bad yet . . . I think her fever got higher after Mom left. Mom told me to stay here and baby-sit till she got back with Alisa's prescription. But, Katherine"—his eyes looked really panicked—"that was at three-thirty. Mom said she'd be right back."

I looked at the clock. It was 8:15. For just a second the image of a burned-out, totaled car flashed into my mind—a horror picture straight from one of those awful drunk-driving commercials they always play on TV. But then I thought, *She wasn't drunk. She was up. Douglas said she could talk,* and I made myself shut off my imagination totally, like you switch off a television.

I took a big swig of coffee, and shook my head to clear it. "She must have just gotten held up somewhere because of the rain," I said. "She'll be back soon. I can't believe she's up, Douglas. That's a really good sign. That's *great.* Why didn't you just tell me before?"

"Another thing, Katherine," Douglas said haltingly. "You're gonna be mad at me . . . "

I almost laughed. After that day, it would take some kind of earthquake to make me *anything* at *anyone.*

"What?" I asked. *She's up. She's sober. She's at the store. She's coming home. It's all over.* I was beginning to feel almost giddy.

"I gave Mom our money," he said. "She told me she needed it for Alisa's medicine. She didn't have any cash."

"You gave her our money?"

He nodded again.

"All of it?"

"Well—twenty dollars. We still have thirteen."

I let that register for a minute. At first it seemed bad, but then it occurred to me that it really didn't matter anymore. Why should it matter? It was over—she was up.

I did laugh then. I laughed out loud. "Well, that was sort of stupid, but who cares? We'll have food now. And she'll probably pay you back after she goes to the bank."

Douglas was looking at me strangely. He didn't say anything for a while, and then finally he shrugged. "Yeah," he said. "I guess."

"What do you mean, you guess?" I was beginning to feel impatient. "Aren't you glad she's up? We can eat now. The money doesn't matter. We can go back to our normal lives."

He kept staring at me. "I just hope she comes back soon. I'm just worried she's so late."

I clenched my teeth. "It's not that late," I said. "It's eight-thirty. Eight-thirty is not late."

"No," said Douglas, "I guess not. Look, I don't feel that great. I think I'm going to go upstairs to bed. Is that okay with you? You'll be okay with Alisa?"

I nodded. "Mmm-hmm." I watched him as he stood up, wrapping the blanket around himself like a cloak. He walked to the foot of the stairs, and was already beginning to climb them when I said, "You don't think she's coming back, do you?"

He stopped walking but he didn't turn around. "I don't know," he said to the staircase. "Maybe. Probably. Katherine, I just want to go to sleep."

"Well how come you guys were out in the tree house if Mom was supposed to be right back? Why did you go up there?"

Douglas still didn't look at me. He ran his fingers through his messy hair and looked sideways at the wall. "Alisa wanted to wait there."

I could tell by his voice he was about to cry again, so I decided not to push the point too far. But I needed to understand this one thing before he went to bed. It didn't make sense to me at all. "Alisa wanted to? She hates the tree house, Douglas. Why would she want to—"

"Because Mom is *crazy,*" he said, whispering so loud his voice cracked. "Okay?" He turned around to face me. "She's not just drunk, she's getting to be psychotic or something. And nobody wanted to be here when . . . she came back." Covering his eyes with his hand, he sat down on the stairs.

I set down my coffee mug, and tried to think of something to say.

"I got home," he said after a minute, "they were in the kitchen, and Mom was telling Alisa all about some man who killed himself by jumping down an elevator shaft. Then she said that *she* didn't want to be alive anymore either. And there's Alisa just sitting there—burning up—*listening* to this. I'm sorry but I think that's crazy. I'm sorry. I want Mom to be better too, but I just don't think it's going to happen."

I stared at him. Then I said stiffly, "Sorry. Good night, Douglas."

"I just don't," he said again, wiping his eyes and beginning to look embarrassed. "I *want* her to. I want our plan to work and everything. And I want Alisa to be okay. . . . Do you think Mom's going crazy? I mean, do you think people do stuff like that just from being an alcoholic?"

Somehow Douglas always managed to make me feel sorry for him even when I was mad at him. This was just exactly like him, to spit out what he really thought in one big outburst, and then instead of sticking by it, to feel terrible and start practically begging me to forgive him for thinking it in the first place. Like it was his fault. Douglas always thought everything was his fault.

I sighed, irritated. I didn't know the answer to his question. Anyway, there was nothing we could do now except wait. We couldn't make any more decisions till Mom came home . . . or didn't.

"How should I know, Douglas? You should go to bed; you look awful."

He did look awful. He looked as sick as Alisa, and I wondered if he was catching what she had. I didn't think I could take it if he apologized one more time, so when he hesitated I said very strongly, again, "Good *night*, Douglas. Go to bed—I don't want you to start puking all over the place too."

He nodded weakly. "Yeah." Finally he wrapped the blanket tight around him and shuffled upstairs, with the banister creaking under the weight of his hand. A few minutes later I heard him run from his bedroom to the bathroom and throw up.

Great, I thought. *A housewide flu epidemic—that's just exactly what we need.*

But then I thought, *Mom's coming back. She's coming back with medicine, so it doesn't matter.*

After that I stopped thinking. The house was finally quiet, so I settled back on the sofa cushions to wait for my mother.

Chapter Eight

She came at midnight. I'd fallen asleep waiting on the sofa, but I jerked awake the second her car pulled into the driveway. It was a terrible jerk, because the dream it had interrupted was so good I'd almost forgotten everything that was going on.

The beginning of the dream got jumbled up in my mind as I came awake, but most of it was still clear. I'd been with Alisa, Douglas, and Tracey in a snowy forest. We were wrapped up in army blankets and sitting on sleds underneath a lamppost like the one in Alisa's drawings. The flame in the lamp was like the one in our tree house. Alisa was in my lap, and we were waiting for someone to come get us—someone who was supposed to take us away where it was warm. This person—whoever he was—was coming through the woods to meet us at the lamppost. We heard his footsteps. They sounded heavy like an enormous animal's as they crunched in the snow. As they got closer, I realized it was probably Alisa's lion king—Aslan—who was coming. I thought it was funny that Alisa had been right all along about Narnia. I was scared, but relieved too, because I knew that once Aslan got there, I wouldn't be in charge of things anymore. Then suddenly, right when Aslan was about to step into the clearing, we heard a terrible crackling sound from the other side of the thicket, and all the trees started collapsing in splinters under the weight of the hail and snow.

I cringed over Alisa's body and reached for Douglas, but my hands only grabbed at the edge of my blanket. Then with a sickening, dizzy feeling, I realized I was awake, sitting up in the living room and my arms were empty. Douglas, Tracey, and Alisa were asleep in their bedrooms. The clock said midnight. The noise had been real, but it was one I'd heard a million times—the comfortable, rattling roar of our station wagon, crackling over twigs that the wind had blown across the driveway in the rain. It ended abruptly, with a strange crunch.

My heart raced a little as I squirmed around, trying to untangle the lower half of my body from the army blanket. I pushed the blanket off my feet and, without stopping to get a coat or shoes, went out the front door in my socks.

The car was half in, half out of the driveway, parked at a weird angle practically on top of the hemlock tree at the side of the house. The driver's door was open and my mother was inside, just sitting there. She wasn't looking around, or gathering things like she usually would have been with the car stopped. She was just staring straight ahead, with the radio and the seat belt buzzer blaring.

"Mom?" The cold air jarred me awake as soon as I stepped outside. I edged around the back of the car to the driver's side, since the hemlock was blocking my path from the front. It had stopped raining, but the ground was still slippery and wet, and my socks absorbed the icy water from the cement driveway, making my feet sting.

My mother jumped when she heard my voice. Her whole body jerked, and she spun around to look at me. "Oh . . . ," She faltered. "Katherine, don't *do* that. You scared me to death." She turned the key in the ignition, shutting the noise off. Then she rested her elbow on the steering wheel and put her face down in her hands. I waited for her to straighten back up but she didn't. I noticed she had an ugly raincoat on—one she hadn't worn in years. Her hair was greasy. Then as soon as I noticed, I felt guilty. *Who cares what she looks like? At least she's awake. Just shut up,* I told myself.

"Sorry," I said, rubbing my eyes. "I couldn't get around the front of the car because of the tree."

She looked up then, and seemed to notice the tree for the first time. Its soggy branches were splayed all over the left side of the hood. She stared at it and her face looked all stricken, like someone had just told her a really nasty lie and she didn't believe it.

"What are you doing here?" she asked, not looking at me.

I shifted from one foot to the other, confused. Where was I supposed to be? My feet in their ice-socks were turning numb. "I just came out to help you carry stuff. Groceries, or whatever." I glanced behind her and saw that the passenger seat was covered with brown paper grocery bags. I looked for a white wax bag like the ones they give at the pharmacy, and finally located it sticking out of one of the grocery bags.

"I mean, what are you doing here this *late,*" she said absently, still staring straight ahead. Then she smiled ruefully, and her eyes got teary. "But I should have known. You're always so good. Such a good baby. My Raggedy Annie Katherine doll."

My throat closed up, and suddenly my face felt icy too. My mom never called me baby names unless she was drunk. She was drunk now. She'd been drunk while she was driving. She wasn't better at all; she wasn't really up.

I didn't try to make any conversation after that. I just turned all my attention to the grocery bags and started carrying them into the house, three at a time, feeling dizzy but oddly resigned. I just wanted to get the groceries and my mom safely inside the house so I could go back to sleep and keep dreaming about Aslan. I thought I understood Alisa a little better. If believing in Narnia made her feel as relieved as I'd felt during that dream, maybe she wasn't so stupid for clinging to it—even if it wasn't real.

My mom wanted to talk, though. Following me into the house on the third trip, she sat down in a kitchen chair and watched me unpacking the bags. Four were full of groceries, five were bottles. White bottles, green bottles, octagonal and barrel-shaped. Vodka, sherry, something brown I didn't recognize. I didn't care. I packed the groceries away first, taking careful stock of what there was. Two loaves of bread. Five two-liter bottles of ginger ale, Life cereal . . . that was Douglas's favorite. Cookies, saltines, ice cream. There weren't any vegetables at all. Two gallons of milk—that would have been good, but the cartons were warm and coated with condensation. The ice cream was totally soft and squashed. My mom must have been blasting the heat in the car—and even still, she must have been driving around for hours for the ice cream to get that melted. I stuck it all in the refrigerator and freezer anyway, making a mental note to test the milk the next day to make sure it wasn't spoiled.

Once the food was put away, I carefully folded all the paper bags and lined up the liquor bottles on the counter like toy buildings. Like a city from the future.

"Katherine, sweetie," Mom said, "we need to talk for just a little while. Since you're up. Okay, baby? Just a little while, and then I have to go to bed too."

I stood with my back to her, tracing the edge of one bottle with my fingernails.

"Would you like a little drink?" she asked cheerfully. "Why don't you get us some glasses. It'll help you sleep. Can't you get to sleep?"

Numbly I pulled two juice glasses out of the cupboard and put them on the table. She pulled another bottle out of her purse, a miniature, and filled both glasses halfway. "You'll like this kind; it's sweet. It tastes like peach." She smiled again, and her eyes filled up with tears. "I guess you're old enough. It's hard to believe you're all grown up and in high school. Sweet sixteen . . . it seems like yesterday none of you kids were even *born* yet. You know, I *had* you when I was only nineteen."

"Fifteen," I whispered, sitting down. I kept thinking about Aslan. It would be nice if there was a real king and he was in charge. But there wasn't. Obviously.

Mom glanced up with a little frown. "No, honey, nineteen. Of course I was *pregnant* at only eighteen. I was barely out of high school when I met your—"

"Fifteen," I said again. "I mean, *I'm* fifteen. Not sixteen."

She took a long drink from her glass, looking irritated, and filled it up again. "Well," she said, smiling again but not as warmly, "you're so grown up it's hard to keep track. Your father always said you were six, going on thirty." She took another drink.

I took a sip of mine too, and coughed. It didn't taste like peach at all—it burned my lips and tasted sour, like chemicals. "Mom, I really have to go to bed. I *am* tired now, I just couldn't sleep till you got home . . ."

"I know," she said, and suddenly there was a hard edge in her voice again. "I know, honey, but wait. I need to tell you about Alisa. Okay, baby? I took her to the doctor, and we got her amoxicillin . . . it's over there on the counter. But Alisa has more problems than the flu right now, and I can't . . ." Her voice trailed off. She pressed her fingers against her lips, looking sad and scared and angry all at once, and then she filled up her glass a third time. "I need your help, Katherine." She looked at me again. "Sweetie? You need to be grown up. You need to be as grown up as you know how to be. Even more than *fifteen.*"

I stared down at the tabletop. She didn't say anything else, so I nodded. I took another sip of the drink, but more carefully so I didn't cough. It went all the way down this time, and burned my stomach instead of my lips. The *aftertaste* was peaches, I noticed. That must be why they called it peach.

"I had to go pick up Alisa at school today," said my mom.

I nodded again, watching the liquid in the glass. This was the first time I'd ever drunk anything alcoholic, besides one time when Douglas and I split a beer in the tree house. The beer had tasted terrible. This peach stuff was horrible too, but it was sort of fascinating in a way.

"The principal told me she didn't want Alisa coming to school anymore till she's evaluated by a psychologist. You remember the principal, Ms. Haley?"

I remembered. She'd been the principal when I was there too. She was a black lady with gray hair and a round, pillowy body, and a laugh that made everyone like her even though they were scared of her. She called everyone "child," even the sixth-graders, and she always wore purple and lots of scarves and big, shiny earrings. I'd always thought she was way too nice to be a principal, but the rumors around school were that she wasn't that nice if you got sent to the office. She was strict. Really strict, but smiley. It was kind of a strange combination.

"She said Alisa's been running away from school," Mom continued. "They've had to track her down three different times, and once she was missing for forty-five minutes, so now they're in this big hubbub. . . . They say they can't keep her *safe.*" She filled the glass again. "Or some such bullshit, and they don't want her coming to school again till she's *evaluated* by a psychologist. I said, How much can it take to keep one little kid *safe*? She weighs all of fifty pounds, for crying out loud—"

"Alisa's not running away," I interrupted, frowning. "She thought she saw something in the woods. It's just her imagination. I mean, I can explain what the—"

"Exactly." My mom cut me off. "There's nothing wrong with Alisa; it's the *school.* I mean, she's having her share of *problems.* Who the hell can blame her, with no father, and me working all the time, and now the job situation—thank you, *Sheldon.*" She emptied her glass and filled it again. "I mean, maybe . . . I mean, welcome to the twentieth century! Show me one kid's mom who can stay home these days like June *Cleaver.* But you know—try to tell that to this Haley woman. She's just all defensive."

"Alisa isn't running away anyway, she just—"

"Of course not, honey, you and I both know that, but it's just this whole spiel about forty-five kids in a *classroom* and the poor overworked *teachers.*" She leaned forward conspiratorially. "You know the whole whiny bit. It kinda makes you wonder where our taxes are going." All of a sudden she started giggling like crazy at that, like she'd made some hilarious joke. She laid her forehead down on the tabletop, and all her hair spilled forward, looking greasier than ever. "I sound like your *father.*" She snorted and started to giggle again. While she laughed, I took the bottle and filled my almost-empty glass up to the top, replacing the bottle quietly so she wouldn't notice. She didn't.

I took as big a swig as I could and concentrated on the burning feeling, wondering idly if the liquid might dissolve my entire esophagus on the way down. When it had settled in my stomach, I said, "So what do you need to tell me?"

Mom looked up, and rested her chin on her arms. "Hmmm?"

"About Alisa? What did you need to tell me before I went to bed? What happened?"

"Oh," she said, and leaned toward me like it was the punch line of her joke. "Well, Ms. Haley gave me the name of this psychologist character, and it turns out he can't meet with us till a week from Friday. He's some honcho for the whole lousy *district.* So . . . so I just need you to stay home a few days and baby-sit Alisa. Okay? Can you be a big girl and do that for me? Just for a few days till we have this meeting and she goes back to school. 'Cause I'm sick too, honey." Her face contorted, and her eyes glazed over with thick, sickly-looking tears. "I'm sick too, and I need to get better so I can take Alisa to the . . . the meeting. So I need your help. It's not fair to ask, I know, but I just . . . I just need your help."

I chewed on my lip and watched a tear roll down her face. Her skin still looked like porcelain, even when she was drunk. "A week from Friday?" I asked. "That's nine days from now. I mean, I'm not saying I won't, I just . . ."

"Oh, Katherine," she said, "I know—I just don't know what else to do. It's hard to be your age and have all this . . . but you need to think of Alisa. Okay? If you won't do it for me, do it for Alisa. You know she absolutely *worships* you."

"I didn't say I wouldn't do it for you. I mean—I'll do it. Fine."

"Fine?"

"Fine." I sat still while my mother walked around the table and kissed me on top of my head, leaning her hands on my shoulders for support. "Good girl," she said, still leaning very hard on my left shoulder. "That's a big relief. You don't know. . . . Do you want another drink before you go to bed?"

I looked at my empty glass, and my chair seemed to rise off the ground and tilt slightly to the left under my mom's hand. I felt like both of us were floating. "No," I said. "No, thanks." I wondered if I was catching the flu too.

"I think I'll have just one more." She sat down again.

"Okay," I told her. "I'm gonna go up to bed."

I walked up the stairs to my room. It was kind of hard to maneuver, but by the time I got to the top, I felt better—just a little dizzy. I went to sleep in my clothes on top of the quilts. I didn't feel cold anymore. The dream about Aslan didn't come back.

Chapter Nine

The next day was Thursday, pouring icy rain, and nobody went to school. Everyone except me was sick. Alisa and Douglas didn't even try to get out of their beds, and when I went downstairs to the kitchen I found Tracey sitting wrapped up in about four oversized blankets like some kind of Egyptian mummy. She didn't have her makeup on and her hair wasn't washed, so I asked if she'd been throwing up too. She didn't answer that; she just said she felt like shit, and she wasn't going to school. Then she put her face down on the table and refused to talk to me anymore. I knew she was telling the truth, because Tracey is such a social animal that she never misses school if she can help it, even though she whines and moans about it all the time. I didn't argue with her, just clunked a glass of water and some Tylenol down on the table. When the school buses came, I told them to go on without us. Then I unwrapped the pink medicine from the pharmacy bag on the kitchen table and took it in to Alisa.

Alisa looked even worse than she had in the tree house. As soon as I saw her sit up in bed, I felt like a total child abuser for waiting so long to give her the medicine. I should have thought to give her the first dose at midnight, but the peach whatever-it-was had made my mind all stupid. Her face was purplish white, her teeth rattled against the spoon, and even though her fever was down to ninety-nine and a half, she still seemed pretty spacy. She slept most of the day, except for the times I woke her up to spoon more pink glop down her throat. Then, at about nine that night, I went to say good night and found her standing, ramrod straight, in front of her closet in white footed-pajamas.

Tracey was asleep in the other bed by then, and the only light in the room came from the orange night-light plugged into the wall. It made a glowing circle on the pink-checkered wallpaper and cast long shadows across the carpet. Alisa stood at the very edge of the shadows, staring intently into the darkened closet. For some reason, seeing her there practically made my hair stand on end.

I asked her what she was looking at.

"I'm tired from walking around the trees," she said loudly. She didn't turn around to look at me. "I can't find the door." Her body was stiff as a board, and I realized she was sleepwalking.

"There aren't any trees," I told her, crossing the room and picking her up. "There isn't any door—it's just a closet. You're dreaming."

Alisa wrapped her skinny arms and legs around me, and as I carried her back to bed, a shiver went down my spine. She hardly weighed anything at all.

"I'm trying to find the door to Narnia," she said into my shoulder.

I sighed. Laying her back on the bed, I gathered her blankets off the floor and gently covered her up again. "I know," I said.

I sat there with her for a long time, stroking her hair and listening to her breathe until I was sure she had settled back into a deep sleep. Eventually I slid down onto the floor and curled up on the carpet next to her bed. The pink-checkered pattern seemed to jump out and hover in the air between me and the darkened wall like a mirage, and after a while I fell asleep too.

I woke up about two hours later to a horrible gasping noise above me. Alisa was sitting bolt upright in bed. Dizzy, I turned on the light, pulled her into my lap, and shook her till her eyes opened. Her face crumpled when she saw me and then she started crying in that awful sobbing way of the day before. It scared me so bad, I felt my skin pricking all over and my muscles turning cold. She didn't want anything to eat, she didn't want a drink, she didn't want me to read to her, or to watch TV or anything. She acted like I was talking to her in a language she didn't understand. She just cried and cried, and her tears made a hot stain on my shirt. Finally she fell asleep again, but I kept holding her anyway.

After that I stayed awake all night. I only left Alisa and Tracey's room twice—to check on Douglas, and to pee. My whole body was shaking.

By Friday afternoon I was so exhausted, I felt like I was going to fall over in a heap, but everybody's fever was down to almost normal, including Alisa's. My mother was back to her usual pattern of staying in bed all day except to go to the bathroom or sometimes get food or ginger ale from the kitchen, so I concentrated on everyone else's problems. Abandoning Tracey's menu, I cooked a whole pot of

SpaghettiOs, using up the last three cans we had in the pantry. Nobody choked down more than a few bites. It occurred to me that they might all have tonsillitis, because I'm the only one in our family who'd had my tonsils out. So after dinner I made them all open their mouths, and I stared down their throats with a flashlight. I didn't know what healthy tonsils were supposed to look like as opposed to diseased tonsils, though, so it wasn't too helpful.

Eventually we abandoned our separate bedrooms and spent the weekend camping out in the living room on blankets and sofa cushions. It was a three-day weekend because of interim grades, which turned out to be a good thing since Douglas had some kind of relapse on Saturday and lost everything he'd eaten the night before. Tracey and Alisa never moved off the sofa; they just lay sprawled under the army blankets, sleeping and sleeping. Douglas played his guitar softly when he wasn't in the bathroom dry-heaving. He was learning some sad-sounding thing, which I guessed was from an old Simon and Garfunkel tape of my mother's but he told me it was part of Mozart's Requiem. I slept, and watched reruns of *Knight Rider* and *The Dick Van Dyke Show,* and listened to the rain falling outside—steady and cold and gray like the entire Atlantic Ocean had evaporated to a spot right over our neighborhood and was plummeting back down again.

Finally Monday afternoon came and the rain slowed to a drizzle. By that time Douglas, Tracey, and Alisa were on their feet with normal temperatures again, but we had two new problems to add to all our old ones.

First, Douglas and Tracey had been out of school for two days without a phoned-in excuse, and I'd been out three. At St. Agnes and St. Luke's, that's a pretty big deal—mainly because of Mrs. Schmiedler, the secretary, who keeps track of attendance for both schools. She is about a hundred years old, and paranoid. According to her rules, your parents were supposed to call the school in the morning if you were even going to be out *one* day. If you were out two days without a phone call, Mrs. Schmiedler would imagine the worst and start calling your house every day to make sure you weren't skipping, or kidnapped, or dying of some terrible disease. We'd stopped answering the phone the first sick day, but we knew for a fact that Mrs. Schmiedler had called our house seven different times, because she'd left seven separate messages on the answering machine in her creaky bat-voice, talking too loud into the receiver.

The second problem was related to the first . . . but more complicated. According to what my mom had said a few nights ago, Alisa couldn't go back to the elementary school at *all*—not until she saw this child psychologist on Friday. And like an idiot, I had told my mother I'd stay home to baby-sit, which meant I couldn't go back to school yet—not for four more days.

"I thought we agreed, don't act suspicious in any way," said Douglas. "If you miss seven days of school, that's not exactly unsuspicious. You can't be absent that long unless you have major surgery or something . . . and we don't even have excuses for *last* week."

"No kidding," I said, irritated. We were back up in the tree house, smoking for the first time in four days—Tracey, Douglas, and I—and the cigarettes tasted weird. The nicotine was making me feel dizzy but I kept smoking anyway. Douglas had his guitar up there, and was back to his usual Led Zeppelin, picking at the strings in a way that was kind of twangy and annoying. Alisa was in another part of the backyard, where I could see her from the tree house window.

Her jeans and red sweater looked too big for her, and she was swinging on a soggy rope swing, which, I noticed for the first time, was beginning to look very frayed and shaggy after years of us hanging on it.

"Alisa!" I yelled out the window.

She twisted around on the swing to look over at me, upside down. Her hair fell backward from her forehead like an orange flag.

"Get off the swing!" I said. Beside me Douglas twanged another chord on his guitar, and I put my hands over the strings to mute the noise.

Alisa stayed upside down. "Why?" she yelled.

"Because. I'll tell you later. Get off!" It hurt my lungs to shout across the yard.

Alisa hesitated, then, scowling, slowly turned right side up. She climbed off the swing and sat down on the wet grass. Then she flopped on her back like a martyr, making a blue-and-red X on the waterlogged green. I sighed so loud it sounded like a growl. All the maternal hormones that had been charging through me while everyone was sick had pretty much dried up when Douglas, Tracey, and Alisa got better and regained their normal personalities again. I was in a terrible mood.

Tracey and Douglas's problem seemed easier to solve than mine and Alisa's. We could forge a written absence excuse for the last week and say it was from our mother. We'd probably get away with it, as long as Tracey delivered the note in person and explained that my mom had the bug too and was too sick to call in. If Mrs. Schmiedler didn't believe her (which was unlikely, because Tracey was the darling of the entire school, including the teachers), Mrs. Schmiedler could call the house and I'd answer with the same story, since I had to stay home for another week anyway.

We decided to get that part over with first, so Tracey forged the letter while we sat there and smoked. She used a sheet of my mother's lavender stationery, and wrote in lacy script: *Please excuse Tracey and Douglas Graham for their absences last week. Due to a dreadful case of influenza, they could not attend school. Warmest regards, Ms. Suzanne Donavan (formerly Mrs. Graham).* She imitated my mom's loopy signature exactly. She even sealed the envelope with gold sealing wax, which my mother got for Christmas once and never used because it was from Sheldon. Tracey melted the sealing wax with a cigarette lighter, and by the end, the note looked very authentic.

After that we used up most of two hours and a whole pack of cigarettes trying to come up with a solution to my problem. It wasn't easy. We all agreed I couldn't get away with a whole week's absence without a doctor's note or a personal on-the-phone explanation from my mother, especially now that Mr. Dodgson was already suspicious of me. On the other hand, there was nobody else to take care of Alisa all week and we certainly couldn't leave her at home with Mom.

Douglas kept saying, "I wish you hadn't promised you'd stay home in the first place," which wasn't exactly helpful, so I finally told him to shut the hell up if that was all he had to say. Tracey threatened to leave if we didn't stop arguing, and that ended the fight, because Tracey had the temporary power of being the only one talented enough to forge the second note once we figured out what it should say. (Douglas and I both have terrible handwriting, which is the downside of being left-handed or ambidextrous.)

We considered taking turns staying home—Douglas on Tuesday, me on Wednesday, Tracey on Thursday—but Douglas pointed out that if we did that all week, even someone as senile as Mrs. Schmiedler was bound to catch on sooner or later, and then she'd *really* want to talk to Mom on the phone, or she might get Dean Schmidt involved, which would be a disaster. (Marcus Schmidt, who is the dean of both St. Agnes and St. Luke's, is a former football coach, about six foot ten. He's the type that has framed posters all over his walls with pictures of athletes and slogans about self-discipline, and he always wears a suit. Once you're on his shit list, there's no getting off.)

We were smoking the last three cigarettes, and everybody was about to give up completely, when I finally came up with an idea. I admit it probably wasn't the best idea I'd ever had, and maybe it was really moronic, but we were so tired it was hard to think clearly. Anyway, nobody else had a better suggestion and it was the only thing we could agree on in the end. We decided to take Alisa to school with us.

Chapter Ten

"Just stand right behind us and be quiet," I said to Alisa. "You remember the plan? Till we get on the bus, you just stand right exactly behind us and don't make any noise."

Alisa nodded, wide-eyed. We were standing out on the front lawn—Tracey, Douglas, and I—shoulder to shoulder in a kind of semicircle with our backpacks and jackets draped all over the front of us, to make a kind of patchwork shield. Alisa was directly behind Douglas, in the middle—undetectable from the street, we hoped. The school bus for St. Agnes and St. Luke's would arrive in about two minutes. Alisa was hanging on to the back of my blazer with her right hand; her fingers had gotten so skinny during the last week, they felt like bird claws clutching at my back. We'd made her put on an old red-plaid jumper, which almost matched our school uniforms. Not that people who saw Alisa would actually mistake her for a St. Agnes student, seeing as she was only about four feet tall—but maybe if they just caught a glimpse of her, they'd see plaid and not look a second time.

I adjusted my coat in front of me, trying to make the sleeves spread out as wide as possible. "Once we get on the bus, it'll be easy," I said. Probably no one was listening to me, because we'd been over the plan a thousand times, but it made me feel better to rehearse it one last time out loud. "Alisa, once you get down under the seat, nobody will be able to see you. When we get to the school drop-off, it'll be crowded so no one will notice anything, and we'll just hustle you into school to the hiding place. Okay? Alisa?"

Alisa didn't answer, but her fingers squeezed the back of my blazer a little more tightly.

"Here comes the bus," said Douglas.

"We'll get used to this after a few days," I assured everybody.

Tracey made a noise in the back of her throat as the flashing stop sign swung out from the side of the bus. "It's a different driver," she said. "It's a substitute or something."

I squinted to see through the dirty windows of the door. Tracey was right, it was a substitute. A Latino lady with short gray hair, she didn't even look up at us—just jerked the doors open with her right hand and studied a road map in her left. I felt a surge of hope and murmured, "Thank you, God" (which is a habit even atheists can develop from being in religious schools too long).

We moved forward in a cluster and climbed up the steps into the aisle. Only three other kids were in the seats already: Jon Wiseman, who played Dungeons & Dragons with Douglas and usually slept all the way to school (which was what he was doing right then), and Brittany and Louise Gill, who were in the way back, looking out the emergency-door window at some guys across the street.

The Gills weren't usually school-bus people, so I was a little alarmed to see them, but they didn't even turn around and look at us. They wouldn't have condescended to say hi if they had. I was one of the social invisibles at St. Agnes, which was fine with me. It was much better than being a reject, which is a step down from invisible, and makes you a living target. (For instance there's this girl, Lindsay, in my class, who has been tortured and ostracized for years. One time in seventh grade she was sucking on her pen and somehow the end popped off the cartridge so she accidentally sucked all the black ink into her mouth. After that she was labeled a reject forever. People like Louise and Brittany and Marnie constantly teased her in the locker room, calling her Black Tongue and spreading rumors about her sleeping with homeless people—which, if you know Lindsay, is ridiculous. She's scared of her own shadow. And all because of a faulty pen.) There is a very fine line between invisible and reject at St. Agnes; you have to be extremely careful not to cross it, or you'll regret it for the rest of your life.

We stopped halfway down the aisle, and Alisa dove quickly into a seat and crawled down to a crouching position on the floor, on the far side. Tracey slid into the window seat above her, Indian-style so Alisa wouldn't get crushed, and I sat on the aisle. Douglas took the seat across the way. After a few seconds I made myself glance backward to see if anyone had noticed. Jonathan Wiseman was still sound asleep with his mouth hanging wide open, and Brittany and Louise Gill were facing forward looking bored. Louise had a compact out and was fixing her lipstick. I noticed she was wearing pumpkin earrings, and it suddenly hit me that it was Halloween—I'd forgotten all about that.

For just a second a picture flashed into my mind from years and years before—of all of us dressed up for trick-or-treating on the sidewalk, and Mom dressed like Mother

Earth inside the house, stirring hot cider while she passed out Milky Way bars to the other trick-or-treaters. My mother had always loved Halloween. She used to sew our costumes herself and take a million pictures of us to post on her bulletin board at work.

Louise met my eyes over her compact with just a hint of sleepy threat, and I swiveled my head back around.

"No one saw us," I said quietly to Tracey. I didn't whisper because I read in a magazine once that whispers can be more easily overheard than low regular voices. That's fact #139 in my green notebook.

"A little louder, why don't you, Katherine," Tracey snapped. Obviously, the sight of Brittany and Louise had shaken her up. Tracey respected the Gills. Unlike me, she aspired to be like them one day—looking too beautiful for any kind of uniform, and dating all the best guys at St. Luke's and Episcopal Prep. The truth was, knowing Tracey, she would probably surpass the social status of the Gills as she got older. She was already kind of the Sara Whittaker of her class. She and Sara shared a regal quality that people like the Gills can't imitate, but only follow around like stupid guppies.

I decided not to waste my breath talking to Tracey anymore, so I turned to Douglas. He looked pale. He seemed to be thinking hard about something, and then he suddenly emptied all the books and papers in his backpack onto his seat. At first I thought he was going to try to study, but after a few seconds I realized he was just making a mess so nobody would take the seat next to him and see Alisa's hiding place. Sometimes I forget to appreciate how intelligent Douglas is. I took out a French textbook and pretended to study it so nobody would stop and talk to me (not that they would have anyway). I nudged Tracey, who stared at me until she got the hint. Reluctantly she took out a science textbook and propped it open on her lap.

"Nobody's going to believe you're totally engrossed in *The Wonderful World of Stars and Planets,*" I muttered.

"Oh well, I apologize for being less of a nerd than you guys," she snapped.

The bus ride to St. Agnes took about forty minutes. After half an hour the seats were almost all taken, and no one had seen Alisa or bothered any of us at all. I looked down at Alisa and she smiled at me. Her eyes looked happier than I'd seen them in a long time—very blue and sparkly. Her knees were drawn up tight against her chest, and her hands were folded peacefully over her backpack, which rested on her feet. When she grinned, her mouth looked too wide for her skinny face. Earlier that morning, when we'd told her about the plan, she'd seemed more pleased than scared. She said she'd rather be with us than at her school anyway.

The bus stopped at St. Luke's first, as usual. St. Luke's is in a building by itself, but it shares administrative offices with St. Agnes, which is down the street. Douglas waited till the rush of boys had stampeded down the aisle; then he gathered his stuff and stood up slowly, running his fingers over his hair and pulling at his earring.

"Good luck today," he said quickly. He hoisted his backpack onto his shoulder and gave me a goofy, nervous thumbs-up sign. Then he walked down the aisle and off the bus without looking back. I was sorry to see him go. Those days, I felt more and more uneasy when we were all separated, even just for school.

The bus lurched forward again, sputtering the last half a block to St. Agnes, and as we approached the bus stop, a nervous pain shot all through my body so violently I felt like I had to pee. Tracey was still staring blankly at *The Wonderful World of Stars and Planets,* but I noticed her bitten-down fingernails were purple and white from pressure. "You remember what to do?" I asked quietly.

Tracey nodded. I looked down at Alisa and raised my eyebrows. She nodded too. She wasn't smiling anymore.

"If we get separated, just check the hiding place after second period," I told Tracey for the third time that morning. "I'll check after first and third and I'll meet up with you at lunch. And don't forget to go by Schmiedler's office and give her the absence notes." Tracey nodded again, and the bus engine cut off.

The plan was not to move until everyone else got off the bus, but Karen Vildicchio, one of Tracey's ten million friends, screwed it up right away. She stopped in the aisle beside me and leaned over me like I wasn't there, tugging on Tracey's blazer with short glittery fingernails. "Hey, Tracey!" she said excitedly. "Trace! I didn't even see you there!" Her breath smelled like cinnamon gum and her shiny leather shoes clicked back and forth in the aisle. She obviously didn't even care that she and her humongous backpack were taking up the whole aisle and blocking everyone else's way. *Very gutsy for an eighth-grader,* I thought. But then looking at her face, I realized it was more than just guts. Karen Vildicchio was one of those lucky people who goes through life oblivious to the dangers around her.

She leaned one elbow on the seat in front of us, and snapped her gum excitedly with sparkling eyes. "Are you ready for the test? Were you sick? Listen, I have to tell you something about Brian's Halloween party. I'll tell you on the way to homeroom—c'mon!" She tugged playfully at Tracey's sleeve again, and her eyes slid sideways to acknowledge me, half apologetic but friendly. "Sorry." She grinned. "Can you let Tracey out?"

I didn't move. Tracey hesitated a second, then pulled herself up until she was standing on the seat and hopped gracefully over Alisa's head into the empty seat in front of us. That caused Karen to burst into hyena laughter so loud I thought my left eardrum would rupture. Tracey laughed too, almost as loud. She jumped into the aisle and hooked her arm through Karen's, tugging her forward as I threw my jacket over the top of Alisa's head. "Bye, Katherine," she called over her shoulder. "See you at lunch?"

"Uh-huh." My heart was pounding so fast, I thought for sure I would have a stroke right then and there. But Karen obviously hadn't seen Alisa, and after a few seconds I let myself breathe again. Everyone else filed down the aisle without taking any notice of us. To my amazement and gratitude, even the bus driver hopped out before we did, without making the normal seat check for forgotten backpacks, jackets, and garbage. In less than two minutes Alisa and I were left alone, and I could see through the window that the sidewalk outside was mostly empty, except for a few smokers hiding behind the Dumpster and having one last cigarette before the bell rang for homeroom.

Taking Alisa's hand, I almost dragged her off the bus before anyone could come out of the building and spoil our chance. I lifted her down to the street and we ran across the sidewalk, taking a sharp right into the alley full of Dumpsters and heating units, and heading behind the school to the doors that led into the gym.

I pushed open a door cautiously to make sure the gym was empty. It was. The lights were off, and the air smelled like floorwax and new basketballs. I pulled Alisa inside and let the heavy door fall shut behind us. The noise reverberated up into the rafters, where all the felt championship pennants were hanging in the dark.

"I didn't know the lights would be off," I whispered. "They'll come in and turn them on for first period."

Alisa squeezed my hand tighter.

"Did you bring your flashlight?"

"Yeah," she said softly.

"Are you too scared? Do you think you can stay in here?"

"Yeah."

"Yeah to which? You're too scared or you can stay?"

"I can stay," she said.

I squeezed her hand from gratitude, and we crept across the squeaky gym floor to the far side, where the bleachers were pulled out and still covered with jackets and leftover soda cans from last night's basketball scrimmage. "Can you get your flashlight out?" I asked.

"Yeah." She must have already had it in her hand, because she clicked it on and right away a beam of light shot into the darkness. We ducked under the side of the bleachers and crawled underneath, where they made a dusty cave. There wasn't room for me to stand, so I crouched down on the floor. Alisa sat down beside me, and dust bunnies scurried in all directions.

"Okay," I said, suddenly feeling very guilty. The hiding place was a lot scarier than I'd imagined it being. "You have your flashlight. And you have your books? And your lunch?"

Alisa nodded solemnly in the dim light and held up her backpack so I could see it. The first bell for homeroom rang, and I started so violently I smacked my head on the bleacher above me.

Alisa tugged the edge of my skirt. "Don't be scared, Katherine," she said quietly. "I won't get caught. I'll see you at lunchtime."

"I'll come back before then. Tracey and I are going to check on you every thirty-five minutes, between our classes."

"I know the plan," said Alisa. "It's okay. You should go to your class."

I don't think I could have left her there alone in the dark except for the next thing she did, which was shine her flashlight under her chin and cross her eyes so she looked like a monster. "H*aaaa*ppy Hallow*eeeen,*" she said in a silly spooky voice. Then she laughed. It was the first time I'd heard Alisa laugh since she'd gotten sick, practically a week before. I promised myself that as soon as we got home from school, I'd help her make a costume and take her around trick-or-treating.

"Go-*ooo* to-*ooo* cl*aaaass*!" said Alisa, still trying to make her voice sound ghostly.

"Okay," I said slowly. "Okay. I'll see you soon. Don't worry."

"I'm *not* worried," she said.

"I'm not either," I lied. And I left.

French class was torture. It was bad enough under normal circumstances suffering through forty minutes of intelligent dialogue like *"Bonjour, Monsieur Raton. Comment ça va?"* (Good morning, Mister Mouse. How are you?) *"Ça va bien." "Comme ci, comme ça." "Terrible!"* (Doing well. Doing so-so. Doing terribly!) *How many problems can Monsieur Mouse possibly have?* I wrote the question in the margin of my French textbook and then erased it carefully.

I screwed up my recitation so bad that Ms. Halvert kept me after class to give me a practice tape, *Monsieur Raton à la Sienne.* She suggested I take it home with me so I could listen to it in my spare time. Of course I couldn't say no, so I had to stand there while she spent about an hour rewinding it for me in her hundred-year-old tape recorder. By the time she handed the cassette over, the bell was already ringing for second period and I'd missed my chance to check on Alisa.

Algebra II was hellish, and chemistry was even worse because I'd forgotten all about the test I'd missed the week before. Mr. Hodges was having some kind of anal-retentive conniption fit about getting his interim grades submitted on time, so I had to sit in the back of the room and take the makeup exam during class. By that time I'd forgotten everything I'd memorized, so most of the identification questions I just left blank. It bothered the hell out of me failing that test. Usually I get A's in science. There was one page I had to leave completely empty. The last question on it was *What is* ATP? I stared at the question for the last two minutes after the bell rang and finally wrote, "Something an Indian lives in," so there would at least be some writing on the page. My hands were shaking as I laid it on the corner of Mr. Hodges's desk, and I practically ran out of the chemistry lab to make it to study hall on time.

Finally, at lunchtime, I headed for the gym, walking the wrong way down the hallway as everyone else flooded toward the cafeteria at the other end of the school. I'd been temporarily distracted by the chemistry test disaster, and as my thoughts returned to Alisa, my throat tightened to almost choking. *She's fine,* I told myself. *She's fine. Tracey checked on her after second period. She's just been reading her Narnia books this whole time; she's fine, she's fine* . . . I started to run, since the hallway was deserted.

I ran into Tracey just as I got to the gym doors. She was coming from the middle-school lunchroom, which was on the other side. "How's Alisa?" I panted. "How was she when you checked on her?" I pushed the closest door inward and saw that the gym was empty. That was good, because I hadn't thought about what we'd do if it wasn't.

"She didn't tell you?" said Tracey, automatically kicking off her shoes before we crossed the gym floor.

I stopped to duck under the volleyball net. "Tell me what?"

Tracey went around the net. "I couldn't check—I couldn't get away from everybody. We had a Halloween party second period, and I couldn't get away from all my friends. I tried."

I stopped walking. "You couldn't . . ."

Her face flushed. "You and Douglas don't know . . . you don't have friends. It's not that easy to lie. Everybody wants to know how come I wasn't at Brian's party last week, and now they're all mad at me. What am I supposed to tell them?"

I stared at her, incredulous. Then I shut my mouth and started walking again. I absolutely hated Tracey at that moment, and I couldn't think of anything mean enough to say.

"Sorry," said Tracey, a step behind me. Not really sorry, though. Sulking.

"I can't believe you're even *related* to the rest of us," I spat.

We came to the bleachers and I ducked underneath. "Alisa?" I called gently. There wasn't any answer. "Alisa? It's us . . ."

Tracey ducked down too, and the two of us stared into the darkness. I kept waiting to see Alisa's flashlight go on, but it didn't. And as our eyes adjusted to the dim light, we could gradually see what we didn't want to believe. Empty shadows and dust. Alisa wasn't there, and her backpack and all her stuff were gone.

After a few seconds we straightened back up and looked at each other.

"Maybe she just went to the bathroom," said Tracey. She sounded scared. "We shouldn't panic. She was here after third period when you checked, right?"

"I didn't check after third period," I snapped.

"You didn't check? *You* didn't check?"

"No, okay? I didn't. I had a *test,* not just a stupid *Halloween* party I couldn't get away from."

"So you didn't check either. And you're blaming *me*?" Tracey's voice rose to almost a shriek. "That is so typical. This whole thing was *your* idea—and you—"

Right then a door closed behind us, and the metallic slamming noise echoed through the gym, cutting off Tracey's sentence in the middle.

My heart jumped. I thought it might be Alisa, but Tracey looked first and I could tell by her face that it wasn't. Whoever it was, it wasn't good.

I made myself turn around. Across the gym, Mr. Dodgson stood leaning against the door with his arms folded and an unreadable expression. He watched our faces for a minute without speaking. Then finally he sighed.

"Have you two, perchance, *lost* someone?"

Chapter Eleven

Even a few days later, when I thought about that moment in the gym and everything that happened after, it seemed so much like a nightmare I couldn't quite believe it was real. I sometimes wondered if I'd finally gotten the flu after all and dreamed the whole disaster. But it had been going on way too long to be a dream, getting more awful and more complicated from the moment Mr. Dodgson found us, and I couldn't wake up from it.

I think the very worst part was following him all the way from the gym to his stupid classroom at the opposite end of the school. It seemed like an hour we were trailing him down the squeaky, deserted halls, totally silent except for the clicking sound of his new shoes and our quieter footsteps behind him. We had to cut through the empty chemistry lab to get to the religion classroom, and as we wound around the stone experiment counters lined with Bunsen burners, dodging wooden stools and inhaling the leftover smell of chemicals I saw a bunch of corked jars all in a row. Each one had some kind of animal specimen lying dead by an etherized cotton ball inside—frogs, a brown toad, and a tiny, perfect mouse that looked asleep. For some reason, my imagination added an extra jar to the picture. Instead of an animal trapped inside, I imagined Alisa, shrunken to six inches tall like the little girl in *Alice in Wonderland,* still alive but breathing poison and trying to climb the slippery walls to escape.

Mr. Dodgson opened the door to his classroom for us, so we had to walk in front of him to get in. My heart was racing, and I could feel my neck and face prickling to splotches as I looked around the room. There was no one else in there and no sign of Alisa. Not a backpack or a flashlight or anything, just empty desks.

Mr. Dodgson pulled two chairs out and set them in front of his desk. "Have a seat," he said.

Tracey didn't move. She didn't uncross her arms or change the cold stare on her face. That made me feel better. I stayed standing too.

"Where's our sister?" I blurted out. I couldn't stand it anymore—him not talking to us. It was like some kind of psychological torture. "What did you do, call the police? Is she with the police? Because I'm in charge of her, and I don't have time for this shit right now. I have to find her." (I almost said, "I don't have time for this shit now, *sir.*" Which would have been really ironic, considering we were probably going to get expelled any minute.)

Mr. Dodgson looked searchingly into my eyes for a minute, then Tracey's, and then slowly shook his head. He took his glasses off and rubbed his eyes, taking a breath like he was about to talk, but he didn't say anything. He sighed instead, a long exhausted sigh.

He's disgusted, I thought. *He probably thinks we smuggled her to school for kicks. The hell with him.* "Where—is—my—

sister?" I repeated in a really mean voice. I was surprised at how mean—and how unafraid, too. "Just give her back to us and we'll leave."

Finally Mr. Dodgson spoke. "And then what?" he asked quietly.

"What?"

"And then what?" he repeated. "What will you do *after* you leave?"

I wasn't sure what he meant by that. I looked sideways at Tracey, but she wasn't any help at all. She just stood there, staring at Mr. Dodgson with such cool-eyed hatred, everything around her seemed to turn to ice.

"I don't care," I finally said, meeting his eyes again. "If you mean detention or something, you can give it to us every day for the rest of our lives if you want. Or go ahead and expel me. But we need our sister *now.*" I'd never talked to a teacher like that in my life. I'd never realized how much of a psychological edge it gives you when things are so bad, they can't get worse.

After a few seconds of silence Mr. Dodgson cleared his throat. "I see," he said. Even though he was speaking quietly, he was starting to look almost as angry as I felt. "Well, Katherine. And Tracey. Regardless of whether *you* care or not, I see that I am going to have to make a decision here. And *I* care very much about whether my decision is right for all parties concerned." He began to rummage around at his desk, infuriatingly slowly, like the key to whatever he was going to do next was written on one of the papers there or something.

Tracey kept her arms folded and drummed her fingers lightly against her upper arm while she stared at him. Her eyebrows rose slightly—just a fractional movement. After living with her for thirteen years, I knew exactly what that expression meant: *I'm not afraid of you. Just looking at you makes me ill.* It was one of her most common looks.

Mr. Dodgson rummaged around some more, without seeming to find whatever he was looking for, and finally dropped the stack of papers he was holding back onto the desk with a bang. Whatever his decision was, he seemed to have made it. "Your sister Alisa and I had quite an interesting conversation this morning," he said.

I felt my blood pressure drop.

He cleared his throat again and kept talking. "No one besides me knows of her presence here—yet." The "yet" stood out of the sentence like a threat. "I wanted to talk with you first. And that is what we are going to do. First, you and I, Katherine, and then you and I, Tracey, are going to sit down individually and discuss this situation"—he looked at me pointedly—"like reasonable people. Now. Tracey, you will go back to class until I call you later. And Katherine, you will stay here so that we can continue this conversation and perhaps get around to the whereabouts of your youngest sister." He sat down in his chair, folded his arms across his chest, and stared us down without flinching, bushy eyebrows set in a straight line. After thirty seconds or so of silence, my psychological edge was gone and even Tracey had looked away. The last lunch bell rang.

After he'd sent Tracey back to class, Mr. Dodgson announced that we were going to his office. He didn't even ask me whether I minded missing class.

"The other religion faculty will be teaching this period," said Mr. Dodgson, "so the office is empty. I can make us some tea or coffee. Do you drink coffee?"

I didn't answer him, even with a look, but I walked with him toward his office. It was smart to divide Tracey and me like that. How could I be sure she wouldn't tell him a different story than mine? I'd have to get to her in between somehow.

"I'll write you a pass, to excuse your lateness now for sixth period. English, isn't it?"

The fact that he was suddenly trying to be nice was about enough to make me puke on the floor. Ignoring his question, I reached the door labeled RELIGION FACULTY ahead of him and pressed my face up to the window to scan the cluttered office for signs of Alisa. There was nothing in there but two metal desks cluttered with papers and coffee mugs, and mountains of stacked books leaning, half-toppling everywhere. It looked like a library after an earthquake.

I was wondering whether I ought to just refuse to go in, and instead call the police, when my eyes caught a little movement behind one of the book stacks. I looked again, harder. Alisa *was* there, sitting on a folding chair. She'd been practically right in front of me, but her jumper blended into the stacked books, making her disappear like a chameleon. I yanked the door open and practically ran into the office.

She was leaning over a picture calendar, which was spread out on her lap with Magic Markers rolling all over it, in rainbow colors. She looked up quickly when the door opened, but she didn't seem startled. In fact, she seemed happier and more relaxed than I'd seen her in a long time. Her cheeks were flushed—until she saw me. Then she started to look pale again.

"Hi, Katherine," she said softly, looking back and forth from me to Mr. Dodgson. "I came out to find the bathroom, but I got lost. He caught me in the hall." Her hands had frozen around her Magic Markers. "He let me look at his Narnia calendar. He said I could color on it. Are you mad?"

I didn't say anything. I wanted to hug and scream at her

at the same time. Mostly I wanted to grab her away from Mr. Dodgson before any more damaging information could come out of her mouth. Maybe it wasn't too late. A kind of frantic hope started inside my stomach. If she hadn't told him much, there might still be a way out of all this. I could apologize for my rudeness and offer to do extra work for Mr. Dodgson after school. He'd have to admit I'd always been a good student up till then. He might decide to give me a break, if he thought it was just a prank. We could go home.

"Katherine?" Alisa repeated, scrambling down off the chair. She didn't look happy now at all. "Are you mad? I didn't mean to get lost." She set the calendar and markers on the seat behind her and most of the markers rolled off onto the floor. "I told him Mommy's sick. He's not mad. He doesn't think it's your fault—he said so. He said you wouldn't get in trouble. He promised. He's going to help us."

He's going to help. Help us? Oh, no . . .

The hope in my stomach flopped over and prickled into nothing. *I told him Mommy's sick.*

He knew everything, then. All of a sudden I could feel Mr. Dodgson's presence behind me in the office like a looming monster.

Alisa clutched the corner of my blazer and said louder, like I must not have heard her the first time, "He said it's not your fault." She looked past me at Mr. Dodgson for confirmation. "Right?"

Mr. Dodgson cleared his throat, and when he spoke, his voice was softer than I'd heard it before. "It's nobody's fault, Alisa. There are things your sister and I need to discuss, that's all. Perhaps you would take your Narnia calendar into the next-door office for now, so Katherine and I can finish talking."

I couldn't speak. Everything—all our lists and plans—was crashing down like card houses all at once and I couldn't do anything but stand there stupidly, swallowing panic as Alisa reluctantly obeyed Mr. Dodgson and let go of me to go gather her markers off the floor. She looked so dejected, I knew I should reassure her. But I couldn't think of what to say. Not with Mr. Dodgson standing right there. My arms felt paralyzed, folded across my chest.

"Alisa," remarked Mr. Dodgson, "you've colored the sunset behind Cair Paravel beautifully. It's much nicer. That was what the picture needed."

Alisa glanced up at him and blushed. All her pale nervousness was washed away by pleasure.

"We'll come get you when we've finished," said Mr. Dodgson. His manner was suddenly all confidence and gentleness, I noticed. No nervousness at all.

Alisa nodded shyly back at him and left the office, clutching the calendar and markers awkwardly to her chest. She didn't look at me as she went out—just kept her eyes fastened on Mr. Dodgson and quietly closed the door behind her.

Chapter Twelve

Once the door was closed, Mr. Dodgson took a deep breath and said slowly in his normal voice, "Katherine. Let me make clear at the beginning that I am not *against* you. I have no desire to make your life more difficult than it is already. I do, however, need to know the truth."

I sank down into the folding chair facing away from him and lifted one hand over my eyes for just a minute so I could focus. My brain was pounding like an emergency signal, over and over. *Shit shit shit, think of a plan, think of a plan. Alisa's lying? No, I can't . . . Then what?*

Mr. Dodgson sat down in a creaky chair right in front of me. "I can't help you if you're not honest. You *must* tell me what's wrong."

I dropped my hand to my lap and had to physically restrain my eyes from rolling—what he was saying was so corny. Like something out of a Monday night network movie.

"Alisa tells me your mother's been bedridden for

months," he continued. "She says you're running the house. She's worried about you."

I wished I had a cigarette to slow my mind down, so I could figure out what to do.

"Your mother is an alcoholic," he said.

It was a statement, not a question. And finally I had something to say.

"She is *not.*"

I meant it too. With every fiber in my body, I was suddenly sure Mom wasn't an alcoholic, and I felt terrible for ever having thought she might be. *Alcoholic* was a terrible word, an awful word. My mother was someone who told jokes. She was someone with a lot of boyfriends, someone who made ponytails and peach cobbler. She was beautiful.

"Alisa told me," said Mr. Dodgson softly.

"Alisa doesn't even know what an alcoholic is," I snapped. "She was lying." I instantly felt like I'd betrayed her, so I added, "Well, not lying exactly. She was scared of you. She just doesn't know."

"She knows more than you think," said Mr. Dodgson. "She knows that your mother is in distress. She knows that what she drinks from the bottles puts her to sleep."

I glanced up at him quickly and saw that he was almost smiling, at the memory of what Alisa had said.

"She called it an enchanted sleep," he continued, leaning forward. "Alisa believes your mother is under an evil spell, caused by whatever's in the bottles. She told me that only Aslan can break the spell. Do you know who Aslan is? He's a character in the Narnia books. He has the power to give life because he was willingly murdered by the White Witch in order to bring spring back to Narnia. He gave himself up to the witch as a ransom for the children and animals. Then, when he'd been killed and the curse of winter was broken, he came to life again. Are you familiar with the stories?"

I scowled at him. What in the world had he said to Alisa since this morning to make her trust him so much? She was way too smart to just spill a lot of personal information to a stranger. And why was he smiling? His expression was full of kindness, but the weirdness of a smile in this situation only made the whole thing scarier. "She isn't crazy," I said out loud. "She just reads too much."

Mr. Dodgson laughed. "I don't think Alisa is crazy at all. In fact I think she's diagnosed your mother's problem better than the average psychiatrist could."

"Well, I'm glad you think it's *funny,*" I said. "I haven't read the books. But for your information, a lot of people think it *is* crazy, how she talks, and it's getting her in a lot of trouble. The last thing she needs is for you to encourage her."

He was immediately sober. "Yes, Alisa told me about the trouble at her school. I don't think it's funny, Katherine. I just find it fascinating. The theological implications in Lewis and Tolkien . . ."

I could feel my face getting colder with impatience, and I was glad when he trailed off and straightened back up in his chair, looking embarrassed. "I think I might be able to solve your problem regarding Alisa's school," he said, more formally again. "I assume that's why she's here?"

I didn't say anything, and neither did he. I wasn't going to volunteer any information he didn't already have.

After a minute or so he said, "Or perhaps I'm wrong. Perhaps this was just your idea of a Halloween joke. In which case, I'll stop wasting my time and refer you and Tracey to the dean of students."

"*Yes,*" I finally said.

"Yes, what?"

"Yes, *sir.*"

He sighed. "I meant, please elaborate. Why is Alisa here at St. Agnes, rather than at the elementary school?"

"Because of the psychologist," I said through my teeth. "The principal won't let Alisa go back to school till she and my mom go to see one. And Alisa's too little to stay home alone."

"Alisa told me your mother is at home."

"My mother is sick."

"A moment ago you claimed that she wasn't."

"I said she wasn't an *alcoholic.* She's sick. Just plain sick. That's all—it's not a crime."

"Neither is alcoholism," he said. Like he'd scored some big point.

"My mother," I said slowly, pronouncing each word, "is . . . just . . . sick. She has the flu."

"And tonsillitis," he said, looking at me sadly. "I remember."

We stared at each other for a while longer.

"I *could* write a note to the principal of Alisa's school, asking her to allow Alisa back in class," he said. "Miriam Haley is a friend of mine. It would be enough for her that I'd talked with Alisa and was aware of the situation. I believe she would allow Alisa back in school immediately."

I tried not to show any emotion or interest. "Why would she listen to you?" I said casually. "You're not a psychologist."

"Ms. Haley and I attend the same church. We share a similar philosophy of teaching. If I told her that in my estimation Alisa is better off in school, she'd trust my judgment."

I tried to imagine Mr. Dodgson and Ms. Haley in church together. It was hard to picture, mostly because on TV when white people go to church, it's always with other white people, and when black people go it's with other black people. I'd never been to church myself, except for a couple of times at Christmas and Easter when I was little. My father only insisted on us going to Episcopal schools because he thought they gave you a better education. (Obviously, he'd never visited St. Agnes.)

"Alisa would have to give her word to stay on school grounds, of course," continued Mr. Dodgson. "And I would need more from you."

"More like what?"

"Like honesty. And a promise that if any of you were in danger, you'd let me know immediately."

He had to be crazy if he thought we'd call him. Still, he seemed to be offering some kind of a truce in exchange for information. Maybe if I just admitted some of what Alisa had already told him, he'd think it was the whole story. If I gave him a little, he might be satisfied that he'd done his good deed for the day. And if he'd really talk to Ms. Haley, that would solve so many other problems. "Miriam Haley," he'd called her. It was weird—until right then, I'd never thought about Ms. Haley *having* a first name.

I looked up carefully. "Why should we trust you? Why would you want to help us?"

"Believe it or not, Katherine," he said dryly, "the simple fact that you and Tracey are my students makes me concerned about your welfare. And now that I've met Alisa, all the more so. I understand you also have a brother at St. Luke's?" He waited for me to confirm.

"Yes," I said reluctantly. "Douglas. In ninth grade."

"Ninth grade," echoed Mr. Dodgson, looking sad again,

and far off somehow. "I know how heartbreaking it is, Katherine. I was Douglas's age . . . That is to say, my father was an alcoholic. I didn't see the worst of it. I was off at boarding school, and in those days . . . Well, I know I didn't see the worst. I was protected. But on vacations I would see glimpses. I'd get off the train and . . . my mother would be badly hurt. I never . . ."

All of a sudden he looked at me more intently than he had so far. "Has she ever hurt you, Katherine? Or any of you?"

"What do you mean?" I'd gotten interested despite myself, and for a minute I thought he was talking about *his* mother.

"Has she hurt you? Hit you—or any of the others? It's very important you be honest about that."

With a shock of horror I realized he meant our mom. "N-No!" I stammered, feeling guilty for breaking concentration. "Look, she's not an alcoholic. Not nearly as bad as your father. Alisa was exaggerating. It hasn't been *weeks.* Just a few *days* our mom's been sick. She was feeling really terrible, so she drank a little wine to relax. . . . It's not nearly as serious as you're thinking."

Mr. Dodgson didn't look at all convinced.

"My mother would never *hurt* us," I added, feeling a little desperate.

Mr. Dodgson frowned. "What about food?" he asked. "Who's doing the grocery shopping? Do you need anything?"

A picture of our nearly empty refrigerator and kitchen cabinets flashed into my mind, along with our current cash balance, and I hesitated for a second. The question might have caught me off guard if it hadn't been for Douglas and my green notebook; fact # 210 was firmly written in my memory: *Drinking too much and not feeding your kids counts as child abuse.*

"We have more food than we know what to do with," I said. "We'll be fine." (And we *would* be, I told myself, as soon as we got some money and a way to get to the grocery store. We'd be fine.)

I must have really looked like I was lying, because the skepticism in Mr. Dodgson's eyes deepened, and the whole conversation would have been shot to hell if I hadn't finally found some inspiration. "And," I added offhandedly, "of course my father calls all the time, to make sure we're all right. He's extremely overprotective."

"Your father?" said Mr. Dodgson, clearly confused. "Alisa said—"

"Oh, Alisa doesn't consider him *her* father. Technically, he isn't. Biologically. But he's my father and Tracey's and Douglas's. He lives nearby. And he visits all the time to make sure we're okay."

Mr. Dodgson blushed a little. "Ah," he said. "Of course. Well, I didn't realize that."

Seizing the advantage, I kept going, almost effortlessly. "In fact, he'll be stopping by the house sometime tonight, I think. With food and everything."

Mr. Dodgson seemed to be trying to make a decision again. He'd backed off quite a bit, I noticed. I could tell I was starting to win. Then he asked the question I should have known was coming: "If your father is nearby, why doesn't he take Alisa to the counselor's appointment himself? Why doesn't Alisa stay with him during the days until then?"

I didn't even panic. It was amazing how easily the truth filtered in to become part of the lie. "Well," I said, "because Alisa's not *his*. You know. If he started taking responsibility for stuff like that, my mom might accuse him of being Alisa's real father, and he'd have to pay child support for one more kid. He has to be careful."

Mr. Dodgson sat silently, taking that in, and his face darkened with anger. I thought I'd given myself away somehow, but as I started going over the lie in my mind, trying to find the weak link, he spoke again. "That's inexcusable," he said quietly. "To neglect her for that reason is beyond irresponsible. It's diabolical." And I realized that his anger had shifted to my father.

"Well . . . ," I said, not sure how to react. "They've been divorced a long time. And Alisa's not his kid."

"It doesn't matter," said Mr. Dodgson fiercely. But then he stopped and sighed. "I'm sorry," he said. "It's a particular annoyance of mine. Well, Katherine, I suppose we'd better bring this to a close. The bell will ring soon. I'm going to let you go back to class now, and Alisa can stay in my office for the remainder of the afternoon. I'll have to meet with Tracey tomorrow, as we've run out of time. I have to teach the last two periods, as you know."

Relief made me dizzy.

"Legally speaking, Katherine, I should call Social Services. But if you're honestly telling me things are under control—"

"They are," I cut in. "Totally under control. Today was stupid, I admit. But we just didn't know what to do with Alisa. I'm so glad you didn't call Social Services. They wouldn't have done anything anyway, because things are fine. But they always overreact. They might have split us up or, you know . . . just threatened to. It would traumatize Alisa. For Alisa's sake, I'm so glad you didn't."

"For Alisa's sake, I may yet have to," said Mr. Dodgson sharply. "But not today. I'll keep checking in with you by phone, Katherine. I'm not going to just let this drop. I'll be in close touch with Ms. Haley, and we'll both be monitoring the situation. If I sense any further signs of trouble, I'll have to refer this to the dean, and he'll make the decisions from there. Do you understand?"

I pressed my lips together, trying not to look triumphant. "Fine," I said. And then I corrected myself. "Yes, sir. Thank you."

Mr. Dodgson's face had an expression I couldn't read. I guess resigned is the closest way to describe it.

"Can I go see Alisa, then?" I asked. "Just for a minute, before class starts?"

"On the subject of Alisa," he said, "may I ask how you intend to transport her home? Will you be stowing away aboard the bus again, or have you decided to hitchhike this time, for a change of pace?"

I bristled. "We'll walk," I said. Which was ridiculous. It would take all night to get home on foot. But to tell the truth, I hadn't planned ahead that far.

"Perhaps you would permit me to write a note to the bus driver, asking him to allow Alisa on the bus later today," he said. "It might make life easier, if less interesting."

I could tell he had relaxed, because he was trying to be funny. I didn't see any humor in it, though, and I didn't laugh. "I guess so," I said, and then forced myself to add, "Thanks."

"Of course," he continued, "I suppose you could always forge the note yourself. You seem to be extraordinarily talented in that area."

I looked at him blankly.

"Forgery, that is. Really, quite . . . uh . . . quite gifted."

"I never forged any notes."

"Oh?" he said thoughtfully. "Pardon me, then. I just assumed you had." Seemingly out of nowhere, he produced a folded sheet of lavender stationery and dropped it on the desk. "Your mother must be really something to bother with gold sealing wax in her weakened condition."

Oh, come on. I glanced at the clock. I only had five minutes to see Alisa before I had to go to gym class . . . and then come back to his stupid classroom for religion.

"Fine," I said. "I forged it. Tracey and I did. Out of necessity. I'm sorry."

"Then," he said with a half smile, "you and Tracey will stay for detention three afternoons next week, and we'll consider the matter closed. 'Out of necessity,' I must enforce the rules of the school. And I won't tolerate being lied to for any reason, Katherine. Above everything else, you need to stay honest with me."

Swallowing anger, I kept my face expressionless.

"You may go now, but I expect you to be at your next class in five minutes."

I turned and left. He had a hell of a lot of nerve, giving detention after all that. For the *forgery,* of all things—which technically I hadn't even done. But as soon as I closed the door and stood in the freedom of the empty hallway, my hatred lessened and was replaced by a kind of exhilaration. The detention was a small loss, considering what might have happened. Mr. Dodgson thought he knew the truth, but he didn't really know anything at all. And he was going to talk to Ms. Haley, so Alisa's immediate problem was solved. Tracey and I could coordinate stories that night, so when she met with Mr. Dodgson the next day she'd be sure to tell him exactly what I had—no more and no less.

The whole thing was like a war, really. Douglas and Tracey and I were the soldiers defending my mom. Mr. Dodgson, the rest of the teachers, and the government were the enemy, and Alisa had been the captured prisoner we'd brought back safely. When I thought about it that way, things didn't seem so bad. For the time being all of us, including my mom, were safe. Maybe we'd lost a little ground, but as far as the major battle was concerned, we'd won. And if we could come out on top after a day like this, then we might even win the whole war.

Chapter Thirteen

"Maybe you should have told Mr. Dodgson yes about the groceries," said Douglas. "I mean, since he specifically offered. Even if you'd just said 'We need some butter.' Even just some butter would have helped."

It was more than a week later. My mom hadn't gotten out of bed, and Douglas was still perseverating on the Mr. Dodgson confrontation. Mr. Dodgson had interviewed Tracey the day after he'd spoken with me, and their meeting had gone smoothly. One thing I was learning about Tracey—she was a good liar. Since their meeting, Mr. Dodgson hadn't brought up our family situation at all. He'd treated me fairly normally in class, and I was beginning to hope that if I kept up with the homework and did well on his tests, he'd gradually forget the whole thing. Douglas hadn't stopped worrying, though. He'd analyzed every detail of our conversations with Mr. Dodgson, and he kept turning them over and over in his mind. At first I'd been grateful for his input, but frankly after a week and a half I was getting tired of the whole subject.

I thwacked a Baggie full of frozen dinner rolls over the edge of the kitchen table so they split into twelve pieces, and then began arranging the hunks on a cookie sheet, to thaw in the oven. "Oh yeah," I said to Douglas, "that would be brilliant. 'Everything's *fine* at home, Mr. Dodgson, and no need to be concerned, but would you just drop a few pounds of butter at my locker tomorrow morning? Then we'll be all set.' "

Douglas leaned forward on his elbows at the table and stared morosely at the dinner rolls. "How many are in the package?" he asked.

"Twelve," I told him. "You can have five, Alisa gets three, and Tracey and I get two each."

He shifted in his chair. "You don't have to give me more all the time," he said slowly. "It's not really fair."

"It doesn't have to do with fair," I said. "You look like a skeleton, and Alisa's a little kid. I'm too fat anyway, and Tracey never eats more than four bites of anything, so we don't need as much. It's logical. Stop talking about it all the time."

Douglas didn't answer me, because everything I'd said was true, including the part about me being too fat, and he probably didn't want to hurt my feelings. Instead he stared gloomily at the ceiling, leaning way back in his chair, and said, "It's too bad we're out of butter."

"We have honey or syrup," I snapped, sliding the cookie sheet into the oven and shutting the door with a bang. "Why don't you stop talking about food. You're starting to piss me off. It only makes it worse."

"We only have enough left for three more days," said Tracey. She was outside on the steps, leaning against the open door and smoking. We had the door propped open because the weather outside had suddenly turned almost hot—the thermometer read seventy-one degrees, which felt like ninety after all the November cold and rain. "I took inventory again this morning," she said. "We'll last today and the weekend on the food that's in the house . . . *maybe* through Monday if we're totally careful."

I sighed, still looking at the oven. "Are you sure? What about the saltines? Those should last at least a couple days, if we ration them."

"Mom took them upstairs."

On the rare occasions when my mother came downstairs to eat, she could hardly walk from weakness. She was white as a ghost, and thin and flabby at the same time. I should have been thrilled that she was eating the crackers. So why did it make me hate her instead?

"You should have a cigarette, Douglas," I said. "Nicotine makes you less hungry."

"No, it doesn't," said Tracey. "That's only a myth. It works short-term but you end up eating the same amount in the long run."

I swiveled around to look at her. "How do you know that?" I thought if she had read it in a reliable source, I should write it down in my notebook.

Tracey just looked annoyed. "Who cares *how* I know it?" she said. "It's true. It's a proven fact."

Douglas went out onto the steps anyway, and shook a cigarette out of the pack. I set the egg timer so the rolls wouldn't burn, and then I went outside too. It seemed ironic to me that while we had practically nothing left to eat in the house, we still had cartons and cartons of cigarettes. I'd never realized how much of a stash Douglas had hoarded away for himself.

As I lit my cigarette off the end of Tracey's, I tried to remember when we'd started smoking right there on the steps, instead of only in the tree house. Sometime in the last few weeks, I guessed. It seemed logical, since there was no one to yell at us anyway. At least we'd still never smoked inside the house, and I promised myself that we never would, no matter what. There had to be some rules left in the universe, or we'd all go insane. Besides, the secondhand smoke could give Alisa cancer or something.

"We have to get more money from somewhere," said Tracey. I know you guys are sick of thinking about it, but we'd better make some kind of plans now, or we're going to run out of food totally, and then we'll really be screwed."

I leaned back against the bottom step, grateful for the warmth still trapped in the stone from the day's heat. The sun was low in the sky, and the light looked orange as it lit the treetops across the side yard. The truth was, a plan for getting money had occurred to me a couple of days before, but I didn't like it so I was trying to ignore it. I was hoping someone else would think of a better idea. Or that my mom would finally get up in the nick of time, like in a movie—although that seemed less likely every day.

"How much money do we have left, exactly?" I asked, even though I already knew the answer.

"Five dollars and thirty-one cents," they said—Tracey and Douglas in unison. Five dollars would hardly buy anything at the gas station minimart near St. Agnes, where we'd done all our emergency shopping so far. It might go a little farther at the big grocery store, but that was four highway exits away from our house. I wasn't sure whether it would even be possible to get there on a bike.

"Well . . . ," I said slowly. "I'm going to go upstairs later and try to get into Mom's purse without waking her up. She probably has some cash in there. She had that twenty dollars from Douglas. It's worth looking, at least."

I flicked the ash off the end of my cigarette and waited for them to object, but neither of them looked surprised, and nobody mentioned the word *stealing*, for which I was truly grateful. They just smoked and absorbed the information quietly.

"When are you going to check?" asked Tracey.

"Tonight," I said. "Or, right now, I guess; there's no point in waiting. We need to know. If there's none up there, we need some time left over to think of something else before we starve."

"Are you sure . . . ," Douglas said hesitantly. "Are you sure we shouldn't just call Dad? There must be some way to tell him we need money without—"

"Without what?" I snapped. "Starting a chain reaction that ends up with Alisa in a foster home? What, Douglas? *What's* the way? If you're so smart and you know a better way, then you tell me what it is." I stared him down until he leaned back against the railing, looking deflated and miserable. Tracey shot me a reproachful look and ground out her cigarette on the steps.

"Where's Alisa now?" I said irritably.

"Reading in our room," said Tracey. "She'll probably stay in there till dinner."

The word *dinner* reminded me of the twelve pathetic rolls that were supposed to be our entire meal. A surge of anger overrode my fear, and I stood up.

"I'm going now, then," I said. "You guys keep an eye on the rolls. Make sure they don't burn, or we'll end up with nothing to eat at all."

"Are you sure Mom's asleep?" asked Douglas. "Maybe you should wait till later at night."

"It won't make any difference," I said, hanging on to the railing with one hand. "It could be four in the morning *now*, for all she knows." Still, my feet stayed planted where they were.

After I hesitated a few more seconds, Tracey said not-quite-nonchalantly, "You want me to go with you, Katherine?"

I shook my head. That was probably the nicest thing Tracey'd ever said to me in the history of our relationship. "No," I said. "We'd just make more noise. Thanks, though." Still holding on to the railing, I inhaled one last breath of acorns, soggy grass, and cigarette. I took it all inside me for protection, and said, "Don't forget to take the rolls out of the oven when the thing dings." Then, grabbing the railing on the other side for balance, I swung myself over Tracey and Douglas's legs and went upstairs.

The weird thing about stealing something from someone you know is how simple it is to do. It's so easy, you can hardly believe it, and once you've done it, you wonder why everybody doesn't get robbed blind all the time.

My mother had kept her purse in the same place ever since I was old enough to remember. She hung the strap over the closet doorknob, on the far side of the room. As soon as I cracked the door open, I could see it hanging there in a patch of striped light, which was slanting in from where the sunset shone through the closed window blinds. My mother was as still as a corpse. Her head was back at a funny angle, and I could hear her snoring rhythmically. The room smelled sour, as usual—rotten and biting, like trash when it stays out in the sun. I was coming to associate that stink with my mom's corner of the house.

I had almost hoped she'd be awake or restless, so I'd have an excuse to put off the whole thing till later. But the time to try was obviously right then; there would never be an easier chance. I slipped off my sneakers and left them in the hallway outside. Then, hardly breathing and praying that the floorboards wouldn't creak, I stepped past the door and crossed the room to where the purse was hanging. Standing in front of the closet, I was less than an arm's length from her bed.

I put my hand on the pocketbook, and slowly tugged the zipper sideways. Even the sound of the zipper was loud in the silence. I heard my mother's breathing catch, and her snoring stopped. I froze, my heart beating so fast it made me lightheaded. A few seconds later I heard her covers rustle slightly, and she sighed and started to snore again, a little more slowly.

Hurry up, I thought. *Get the money and get out.*

My hands were shaking, but I managed to unzip the purse the rest of the way and reach in. I had to dig through a lot of other junk to get the wallet—makeup tubes, piles of folded Kleenex, a perfume sample, and flat packs of sugarless chewing gum. The smell of spearmint blended with the leather and the perfume, and I recognized what used to be the smell of my mother in the old days, when things were normal. That almost stopped me, but I made myself keep going. Finally my fingers found the wallet and parted the snapped pocket where she kept her cash. I felt soft paper bills and had begun tugging them out when a terrible noise—the loudest I'd ever heard in my life—split the gloomy darkness and shattered my nerves into a million pieces.

It was the telephone. And it didn't ring just once—it kept ringing and ringing. Screaming, it sounded like. My mother snorted and rolled over on her side to face the phone. There wasn't any time to think. I closed my fist around the money, scrambled out of the room as fast as I could, and shut the door quickly behind me. In the hallway I hesitated, listening. The phone stopped ringing abruptly, and after about thirty more seconds of silence, I heard a soft moan. Then, gradually, I heard her begin to snore again.

I picked up my sneakers with the hand that wasn't clutching the cash and padded down the hallway to my bedroom, where I dropped the sneakers on the floor and collapsed forward across the bed. I lay there for a few minutes, waiting for my heart to stop racing so I could look to see how much money I was holding. When I looked, I could hardly believe it.

Six dollars. That was it. It hardly seemed worth robbing your mother for.

Folding the money, I shoved it in my jeans pocket and buried my face in my arms. Part of me wanted to just stay right where I was for the rest of the night—to crawl under my quilt and not come out. But I was hungry, and I knew Douglas and Tracey would want to know if I'd found any money. They were probably downstairs wondering.

Well. Six dollars was better than nothing. It more than doubled what we had left, at any rate. I made myself climb off the bed and clattered back down the stairs.

By the time I reached the foyer, I could hear Douglas on the phone, which surprised me a little. Douglas isn't the type for social phone calls. It's not that he has no friends, but his friends are the type to call for an assignment or something and then hang right up.

"Yes, sir," I heard him saying. "That's true."

I swung around the corner and looked questioningly at Tracey, who was in from the porch, watching Douglas talk. She had an unlit cigarette in her right hand, and she was rolling it up and down between her fingers. The kitchen was getting chilly with evening air from outside.

"Is it Dad on the phone?" I asked.

She shook her head quickly and signaled me to be quiet, not taking her eyes off Douglas.

"I thought Dad was still in Hawaii," I said stupidly. "Is he calling from Hawaii?"

Tracey made a violent gesture for me to shut up. "Lower your voice, will you?" she whispered loudly. "Douglas told him you weren't home."

"Told *who*?"

"Mr. *Dodgson.*"

I stared at her in disbelief. It had been at least ten minutes since the phone had rung. Douglas was clutching the receiver stiffly, looking green and uncomfortable. I guess I'd known since the day we were caught that Mr. Dodgson might call sometime. He'd said he would—but somehow I just assumed *I'd* be the one to answer.

After a few seconds of paralysis, I grabbed a stray paper towel off the counter, and a permanent marker from the jar of pens by the phone. *Don't tell him anything,* I scrawled on the towel, and held it up a few inches from Douglas's face.

Douglas immediately spun away from me to face the corner, cupping a hand over his free ear. The telephone cord wrapped around his skinny back. "Sure," he said. "Yes, sir, we certainly will. Thanks for calling. We'll talk to you again soon." He was clearly trying to end the conversation, but Mr. Dodgson must have had more to say, because he didn't hang up.

I could feel my blood pressure skyrocketing. I grabbed another paper towel, and wrote, *We will not talk to him soon. Don't encourage him!*

Tracey snatched that towel out of my hand before I could show it to Douglas, but Douglas seemed to be finally getting to the end of the conversation anyway. "Okay, sir," he said. "Yes, I will. Of course. Goodbye."

He put the receiver down and seemed to rest the whole weight of his body on the phone. He shook his head slowly, and without turning around, said, "*Honestly,* Katherine. You make it pretty damned hard to sound normal."

I was a little taken aback by that. It was about the harshest thing I'd ever heard Douglas say to me.

"Sorry," I said quietly. But I was too distracted to stay quiet very long. "What did he want? Why did you answer the phone?"

"I answered," said Tracey. "I talked to him too."

"Well, what did he want?"

She hesitated. After a few seconds she said, "He didn't want anything, I don't think. He was really nice. He just said he knew things were hard here, and if we need anything we should call him."

"He does *not* know things are hard. He's trying to psych us out. I never told him that." I paused, feeling out-of-breath angry. Neither Tracey nor Douglas said anything, so after a while I added, "I hope to God *you* guys didn't."

"Of course not," Tracey said, her voice rising. "We're not stupid."

"What about you, Douglas?" I demanded. "What *exactly* did he say? And what did you tell him?"

Douglas looked at the floor and then said, "He wanted to talk to you and Alisa, and I said you were both out at the library. Other than that, he said what Tracey just told you. I told him things were fine. And he *was* nice. Very nice, actually. He sounded nervous. I think he's just worried about us."

Something about Douglas's tone bothered me. It was like

he was being patient with me. Like he and Tracey both thought I was an irrational lunatic or something. If it was up to them, they'd probably rather tell Mr. Dodgson everything and have him in charge instead of me. I noticed one of the doors under the sink was standing partially open, and kicked it shut—a little too hard, so it banged.

"Well, I hope you didn't encourage him," I said. "If he calls again, you should give the phone to me. Believe me—I'm the one who talked to him that day, and he isn't just *nice.* No one's that *nice,* if they don't have some ulterior motive."

Douglas and Tracey exchanged looks.

"What?" I exploded. "You think I'm paranoid? Well, I happen to be the only one of us left who's thinking about *Alisa,* apparently. *You* guys are the ones who knew Theresa and Jamal. *You* guys are the ones who said the government can take kids away if there's not enough food and stuff. This was just as much *your* idea."

"Katherine," said Douglas slowly, "no one's blaming you. It's just . . . Tracey and I were talking earlier, and at this rate we're all going to starve to death, *including* Alisa. What good will that do her? Plus, what good does it do Mom if we just let her die up there? It's been practically two months. Mom can't go on like this forever, no matter what you read in a magazine. Sooner or later, she's going to die from drinking all that alcohol and never eating, and we'll be responsible because we never told anyone. If we have to tell, maybe Mr. Dodgson would be a good person to help."

"Did Mr. Dodgson tell you to say that?"

"Katherine," said Tracey, "it's just common sense!"

That was too much—to hear it from Douglas was one thing, but not Tracey. I clenched my jaws and said, spitting each word out separately, "We don't *need* help. I can take care of Mom. Mr. Dodgson is a trap. If you tell him anything more, we're going to lose Alisa. And don't say I didn't warn you." Then, turning on Douglas, I demanded, "Where are the rolls? Did you take them out?"

Douglas blanched. With measured rage, I stuck a potholder over my right hand and opened the oven door. I banged the cookie sheet down on top of the stove, and the rolls went rolling everywhere. They were black on the bottom. Carbonized.

"You guys are idiots," I said. "Total idiots. I'm going to bed."

I started to leave the kitchen, and then as an afterthought, I spun around and slammed down the six dollars on the table. I hoped it made them feel guilty. "In case you're interested," I said, "here's the six bucks I just practically risked my life to steal from our mother so you could eat. If you guys are so brilliant, then *you* can figure out how to make it buy enough food so we don't starve to death for another week."

On my way out of the kitchen, I almost knocked Alisa over. She was clinging to the door frame, and I had no idea how long she'd been there. I ran up the stairs and slammed the door to my bedroom. Then I hoisted the window open and smoked a cigarette fast, inhaling deeply so it burned my lungs. I was glad it burned. I smoked five more in a row, more slowly each time until, by the fifth cigarette, I could barely drag the smoke into my lungs anymore and my head was spinning. Then I crushed the last butt out on the windowsill and lay down on my bed, where I eventually fell asleep in my clothes without doing any homework at all. There were no rules in the universe anymore anyway. We might as well just accept it.

Chapter Fourteen

In the morning I felt awful. I woke up about an hour before my alarm went off—wrinkled and dizzy and staring at a pile of ugly cigarette butts on my windowsill. The first thing I remembered was how I'd practically knocked Alisa over the night before. The second thing was that I'd stolen all the money out of my mom's purse. My head ached, and I thought that for the first time I could completely understand why my mother would want to stay in bed forever. But I went downstairs to boil some water for instant coffee anyway.

The downstairs part of the house was freezing, and I wondered if we'd left the door open all night. When I got to the kitchen, I was surprised to find Tracey already dressed for school, standing at the stove and stirring something in a pot. I think she heard me come in, but she didn't turn around.

"It's freezing in here," I said.

She nodded. "I can't tell if the heater is working or not. I think it's broken. I'm making oatmeal for us."

She didn't seem to be mad at me anymore. I went into

the bathroom off the kitchen and filled the metal teapot with water from the sink (the kitchen sink had been useless ever since Douglas had fooled with it that morning). Then I came back and clanked the kettle down on the stovetop to boil.

"I'm sorry I screamed at you and Douglas," I said. I made myself spit it right out, because when you put off things like that, it only makes it worse.

Tracey nodded. "Don't worry about it," she said.

"Alisa heard us arguing," I added, after waiting a few seconds to see if she was going to tack on anything nasty.

"I know," she said. "She's worried about the money. She found eighty-five cents under the sofa cushions and told me to give it to you. It's there on the table."

Three quarters and a dime were piled in a shiny little stack near the sugar bowl. That made me feel worse, not better. Alisa had seemed to be doing okay in school for the last two weeks—at least she claimed she was glad to be back, and she'd promised to stay right by the school building at recess. There hadn't been any more letters home from her teacher, but she was still so quiet it gave me the creeps. Alisa had never been a rambunctious kid or anything, but she used to talk quite a bit. Too much, actually. These days, when she spoke to the rest of us, it was hardly ever about reality—only about what was in the stories she read.

"How much of our fight did Alisa hear?" I asked.

"The whole thing, I think."

"Oh." I sat down at the table, feeling more miserable than ever. "Do you want to go outside and have a cigarette?"

"Yeah, in a minute," Tracey said. "I want to finish this first. I defrosted that box of mini-sausages; we're having those too. With the oatmeal."

Those sausages were the last meat we had in the house,

and I knew it was probably foolish to eat them, but my defenses were down. When Tracey said the word *sausages,* I was suddenly so hungry I felt a little nauseous.

"You said those were supposed to be for dinner on Sunday," I said reluctantly.

"I know," Tracey said. "I changed my mind. I don't think we're eating enough." Her voice got harder then, almost hostile, and she clanked the spoon down on the stovetop, making a mess. That was very unlike Tracey. She's usually neat even when she cooks. "Listen, Katherine," she said. "I was going to wake you up in a few minutes anyway. Douglas and Alisa are gonna be down here soon, but I have something to say first. We can sit here, or smoke. Which do you want?"

I was surprised by that. "To smoke," I said.

"Fine." She grabbed her coat off the hook by the door, turned down the heat under the oatmeal, and went outside without even waiting for me. It took me longer to find my jacket, so by the time I got out on the steps myself, she was halfway through her first cigarette.

"What?" I said.

"Douglas and I were up practically all night, talking," she said. "I wasn't sure last night when we were fighting, but later I decided you're right about Mr. Dodgson. Douglas agrees with me too. We don't need his help."

I was too surprised to know what to say, so I didn't answer.

She handed over her lighter and kept talking. "We can't be divided against each other if we're going to survive," she said. "I was saying to Douglas—the point is for *us* to survive, so that *Mom* can survive . . . hopefully. And anyway, I think we solved the money problem."

"You did?"

"Yeah. *I* did. I think. Here." As soon as my cigarette was lit, she reached in the pocket of her blazer and handed me an envelope. It was addressed to my mother with a return address from my dad. I half recognized it as one of about fifty thousand pieces of mail for Mom that we'd been piling up in a stack in the foyer for weeks. My mother had never opened any of it.

I turned the envelope over in my hands. "It's a letter from Dad?" I said. It was postmarked from Michigan, not Hawaii, so he must have mailed it before he left for the dentist conference. "What—you think we should call him? This is an old letter."

"No, Katherine." Tracey shook her head. She leaned over, opened the envelope, and pulled out what was inside, smacking it back down into my hand.

It wasn't a letter. It was a check for eight hundred and twenty-five dollars. In the bottom left hand corner was written in Dad's barely legible handwriting, *"Child support, mo. of Oct."*

I stared at it for a few seconds before I really grasped what it was.

"You opened Mom's mail," I said slowly. "This check was in the mail?"

Tracey didn't look at me. She hugged herself against the chilly air and smoked fast. "I knew it had to be in there somewhere," she said. "He sends the check every month, right? Mom hasn't touched any of that mail since September."

I looked back down at the check. Eight hundred and twenty-five dollars. Right there in my dad's scrawly handwriting. It was like a miracle from God. "This must have been sitting in the foyer for weeks," I said. "I never even thought of it."

"Yeah."

"That was really smart of you."

Tracey jerked her head in a nod, still not looking at me.

"I wonder how we could get it cashed," I said quickly, thinking out loud. "I don't know if the bank will do it."

"Douglas is gonna ride his bike there after school and deposit it," she said. "I know how. You just have to write 'for deposit only' on the check, and then forge the person's signature. I can do that. Then you say you want to deposit most of it but you need like, fifty or a hundred dollars of it in cash."

"And they'll just give you the cash?"

"I've seen Mom do it a million times."

"Yeah, but are they gonna just give the cash to *Douglas*? Don't they make you prove you're the person on the check or something?" I looked back up at Tracey. She looked beautiful, as always, with her cheeks turning pink in the cold and her hair blowing. She seemed older, though, and the expression on her face was intense. Frowning the way she was just then, she looked a lot like Douglas and me.

"He can prove he's her son," she said. "He can just say his mother's sick and she asked him to go deposit the check for her. That must be allowed. Or what do people do when they can't go to the bank? Sick people, or old people who can't drive?"

I thought about that. It was a good point.

"Why Douglas?" I asked after a while. "I'll do it. I'm older."

Tracey shook her head. "The bank closes at four-thirty," she said. "That's less than an hour from when we get home. You'd never be able to bike there that fast. You're not in good enough shape."

That was true, but it was sort of rude to say.

"And *I* can't," she added, "because I look too young. So Douglas should be the one. He knows already, and he's planning to go. We just wanted to tell you first. And make sure you think it's a good idea."

I forgave her for the out-of-shape comment. "It *is* a good idea," I said, trying not to sound as surprised as I felt. "Really good."

Tracey ground out her cigarette with her shiny penny loafer. "The worst that can happen is they'll say no. But I don't see why it won't work. We should have the money by this afternoon . . . and Douglas and I figured out how we can get to the grocery store tonight, too."

Clutching the check in my hand, I tried to think of a way to say thank you without sounding too stupid. Then I remembered something. "Isn't Karen's birthday party tonight?" I asked. "You can still go to that . . . I mean, if you want. We can wait and go shopping tomorrow."

"I'm not going," said Tracey.

"No, really, I think you should. Douglas can still go to the bank today, and—"

She cut me off. "I'm not *going,* Katherine."

"Why?"

"Because I'm not invited."

I blinked. "I thought Karen and you were best friends," I said stupidly.

Tracey flicked the lighter on and off in her hand. "We were. Now we're not. A lot of people don't like me anymore. I'm not . . . cheerful and stuff, like I used to be. They think I've changed since last year."

"Oh," I said quietly. Tracey had never said anything about that before . . . although it made sense, now that I thought about it. The telephone had been ringing much less often in the afternoons. "I'm really sorry," I said. I really was.

Tracey shrugged. "I don't care," she said. She didn't look at me. "They're mostly jerks anyway."

"They're *all* jerks," I said. "If they don't like you anymore, they're idiots."

Tracey smiled at me briefly. She stuck the lighter in her pocket. "We should go in now . . . there's oatmeal. And sausages." She slipped back into the house and slammed the screen door in my face before I could answer.

After she left, I stayed on the steps for a few more minutes to finish my cigarette. My fingers were cold, but I wanted some time to settle down. It was weird, I thought, how smart Tracey was becoming—all because of Mom. Maybe this crisis would turn out to be good for us. When Mom finally got better, maybe we'd all be stronger people. At least we'd all be on the same side, which had never been true before. We used to fight constantly—at least Tracey and I did—and it drove Mom crazy. It occurred to me that Mom would be proud of us if she woke up and things were still running so smoothly.

Not *if,* I corrected myself. *When. When* she wakes up, she'll be proud.

The smell of frying sausages drifted out the door and I went inside.

If you ever want to experience heaven, you should eat cold, gross food for eight days, and then practically nothing for three more, and then have oatmeal and sausages for breakfast. They weren't really breakfast sausages; they were the little kind that people usually serve as hors d'oeuvres. My mom had bought them to make this fancy pastry-sausage-onion-mushroom thing for Sheldon, but we'd long since used up all the vegetables and pastry dough. Anyway, the sausages were just as good by themselves, and they made the whole house smell homey. There were sixteen in the box, so we could each have four, plus oatmeal. The food put everyone in such a good mood that a truce was automatically declared without anybody saying anything (except Tracey and me, separately outside). The meal was like a victory celebration, even though the victory hadn't technically happened yet.

Alisa cut her sausages into about forty tiny pieces and arranged them in a ring around her bowl of oatmeal.

"How was school yesterday, Alisa?" I asked her. I was trying not to wolf my breakfast down all at once, so I figured I'd slow myself down with conversation and kill two birds with one stone.

Alisa had just speared one of her sausage fragments with her fork, but when I spoke to her, she laid the fork back down on her plate. "Fine," she said quietly, looking at me steadily. She must have known I didn't want to just chitchat about school.

"Keep eating your breakfast or you'll be late. Did you stay on school grounds?"

"Yes," she said, picking up her fork again. She kept her eyes on me so I knew she was telling the truth. (Alisa's eyes were dark blue when she came home from the hospital, and I remember Mom telling us that they'd probably turn hazel or gray when she got older, like ours all had. But Alisa's had only gotten bluer the older she got, so by then they were the color of cornflowers. Not pale, like most people's blue eyes.) I could always tell by Alisa's eyes how she was feeling, and whether she was telling the truth. She didn't lie often, but sometimes she didn't say all of what she was thinking, and then she'd always look down or away from me.

"Good," I said. "I'm sorry about last night—about how we were fighting. I didn't know you could hear us till I walked past you in the doorway. You should have told us you were there, instead of eavesdropping."

Alisa frowned. "I wasn't eavesdropping," she said. "I came to see if supper was ready. And anyways, I could hear you guys all the way from my room." She put a piece of sausage in her mouth and chewed, looking stubborn and dignified. Not even defiant, exactly. More like a martyr.

Tracey and Douglas continued to eat in silence. I could tell they were intentionally staying out of the conversation. I gave up on the eavesdropping tangent. "Anyway," I said, "thanks for the eighty-five cents, but I think you should keep it. We found money from somewhere else, so we don't need cash anymore. And next time Mr. Dodgson calls, I'm gonna hang up on him. We're fine by ourselves."

Then Douglas interrupted. It was the first time he'd looked up from his food to even breathe. "So you want me to go to the bank after school, Katherine? I can get there by four, but I need to know now, so I can cancel with Jake and Jon Wiseman. I was supposed to meet them after school for something."

I nodded, and was about to answer him when I heard Alisa put her fork down with a hard little clunk. She had stopped eating and was staring at me, frowning, with her mouth half open. "Why?" she demanded.

That took me off guard. "Why what?"

"Why are you going to hang up on Mr. Dodgson? Can't he call here anymore? That's the only time I get to talk to him!"

"You didn't talk to him. Douglas did."

"Last time, I talked to him."

"What do you mean *last* time?" I had a terrible sinking feeling.

"Last time he called!" There was a kind of sturdiness in Alisa's face that hadn't gone away even with all the other changes of the last months. Her mouth was clenched into a knot. Stubborn.

"He's called the house before?" I glanced suspiciously at Douglas and Tracey, but they seemed as confused as I was.

"Yes." She clutched the edge of the table with both hands, and her fingers turned white. "Twice. He only wanted to talk to me, those times. You shouldn't be mean to him, Katherine. He's friends with Aslan. Aslan can help Mommy get better. He's the only one who has a cure."

I tried really hard to keep my voice gentle, but I was getting too angry. The niceness came out fake. "Aslan is imaginary, Alisa. He can't cure anything. He's just a character in a book. Now, when exactly did Mr. Dodgson—"

She cut me off. "He is *not* imaginary. Mr. Dodgson says he's real." She shrank down in her chair and folded her arms across her chest while we all absorbed that information in silence.

"He *told* you that?" I said finally. "On the phone?"

"On the phone *and* in his office. A *lot* of times." Then she looked straight back into my eyes. "I believe what Mr. Dodgson says more than you," she said. "I don't think you even know how to make Mommy better. You just always pretend she isn't sick."

She slid down off her chair, leaving half her food on her plate, and walked out of the room in silence. A few seconds later we heard her bedroom door slam, and she didn't come back out again until her school bus honked outside. When she came out, she was fully dressed. She didn't look at any of us or even say goodbye; she just stared grimly ahead of her and marched out the front door. Alisa has excellent posture when she's angry.

Chapter Fifteen

"I heard you called yesterday. I heard you've been calling our house a lot."

It wasn't until fourth period ended that I finally managed to catch Mr. Dodgson. I'd checked his office between every class, and that was the first time he'd been in there at his desk—camouflaged, as Alisa had been nearly two weeks before, against colorful stacks of books. He jumped a little when he heard the door, but when he saw me he leaned back in his chair and motioned with his free hand for me to come in, while he continued to write comments on some student's paper. It was a strangely polite thing to do, considering I'd just barged in without permission. The office smelled like dust and scalded coffee.

I put my hands on my hips.

When Mr. Dodgson finished writing his paragraph, he laid the pen down and looked up at me. "Hello, Katherine," he said. "What a surprise."

I couldn't tell if he was being sarcastic or not.

"There's no need to call my house and talk to all my

siblings," I said. "If you have any questions, you can just ask me directly. You see me in class every day, plus in detention half the time."

"Yes, I do," he said slowly. "But you don't tell me the truth. Not the whole truth, at any rate. And if I don't get at the whole story somehow, I can't help you."

"We don't want help."

"You don't," he said, and sighed. "I believe that. And I believe that Tracey and your brother Douglas are largely in agreement. But you'll have to pardon me for adding that I don't care. Alisa wants help desperately. And even if none of you did, I'd still be compelled . . . *bound,* in fact, to help you."

"I'm sure your contract doesn't say anything about helping Alisa," I snapped. "She doesn't even go to St. Agnes."

Mr. Dodgson smiled. "It's not my contract with St. Agnes that binds me," he said quietly.

I wasn't sure what that was supposed to mean, but for some reason it kind of took the wind out of my sails. I sat down in the chair facing Mr. Dodgson's desk. "I don't know how you can call *me* a liar," I said in a softer voice. I was beginning to feel tired. "You're the one who's lying—telling Alisa that Narnia is a real place. It's not like it helps anything; it just messes with her mind. If you say you care about her so much, then you should encourage her to face reality. She's not a baby anymore. She's almost nine years old."

Mr. Dodgson frowned. "Did Alisa tell you I said that Narnia was a real place?"

I paused, and thought. It's important to have your facts straight when you're trying to win an argument. "She said you believed that *Aslan* was real. She said you told her that *lots* of times, on the phone . . . and in your office. Those were her exact words."

Mr. Dodgson relaxed. "Oh," he said. "Well that's true, then. I do."

"You do what? You do remember telling her that?"

"I do believe that Aslan is real."

I stared at him for a long time.

"What?" I said finally, feeling more tired than ever.

"Well, perhaps I would phrase it a little differently than Alisa," he continued, unruffled. "It might be more true to state that he is real *and* imaginary. Certainly, C. S. Lewis imagined him. Certainly, he is as real as you and me. Real *and* imaginary. But above all else, real." He smiled absently to himself.

The bell rang for the beginning of fifth period.

"Whatever," I said, turning to leave. The last thing I needed was to deal with one more crazy person. "I have a class."

"Yes, yes, so do I . . . but stay a minute, Katherine. For Alisa's sake." Mr. Dodgson's voice sounded so urgent, I stopped. "Here," he said, tipping the pile of books on his desk diagonally, scanning for a title. "Do you remember Alisa's letter to C. S. Lewis?"

Remember? How could I forget? If she hadn't written that stupid letter and run away from school looking for Narnia, her teacher wouldn't have insisted on the meeting with the school psychologist. Therefore, we wouldn't have had to smuggle her to St. Agnes. Therefore, Mr. Dodgson would still be blessedly uninvolved in our lives. He'd just be a nervous, bald religion teacher I could leave behind at school when the last bell rang.

"I remember," I said.

"Well, Lewis received *hundreds* of letters like Alisa's while he was still alive." Mr. Dodgson found the book he was looking for and pulled it from the middle of the stack, causing several of the top volumes to slide onto the floor with a crash. His hand shook slightly as he passed me the book, a thin hardback titled *C. S. Lewis' Letters to Children.* "This book is full of his letters back to them," he said. "He answered every letter he received. Children all over the world read the Chronicles of Narnia. They read about Aslan—a strong, good lion king in a fairyland—and they believed in him in a way that surpassed ordinary fantasy. They fell in *love* with him. There's a documented case in England where a child actually chopped his way through the back of his parents' wardrobe with an ax, trying to get to Narnia." He grinned and adjusted his glasses as he sat back down. "And why? Because Lewis had endowed this king with the characteristics of Christ himself. One of my colleagues at Georgetown is writing a dissertation on—"

"Alisa's not part of somebody's *dissertation,*" I interrupted loudly. "She lives in reality. With me. And I don't believe in God."

"Well," said Mr. Dodgson, chuckling, which annoyed the hell out of me, "that's all right. Neither did St. Augustine, for the first half of his life. Or Paul. Not in the same way, anyway. Neither did C. S. Lewis, as a matter of fact."

It occurred to me that I was trying to reason with a religious fanatic, and that I was wasting my time. Ms. Bledsoe—the one who was the religion teacher before Mr. Dodgson—used to say that the root of almost every war in the history of the world was religious fanaticism in one form or another. She said that human reason was useless in the face of strong religious sentiment. Little did she know her replacement at St. Agnes would be a real live fanatic.

I dropped the book back on Mr. Dodgson's desk. I had made up my mind to leave, but first I wanted to know something. I was already late for class, so I figured I had nothing to lose. "You said your father was an alcoholic, right?" I asked Mr. Dodgson. "You said he beat your mother. Didn't you tell me that?"

The effect on Mr. Dodgson was unbelievable. It was like he'd been soaring above the earth and suddenly fell seventy stories to the sidewalk. "Y-Yes," he said, dropping his eyes and grabbing the right earpiece of his glasses. "Yes, I told you that. Perhaps I shouldn't have. It's really my business alone. I only meant—"

"But you say you believe in *God*?" I demanded. "How did God let that happen? If there is a God, how come he didn't fix your family? How come he didn't save your mother from your father?"

Mr. Dodgson looked sadder than I'd ever seen him, and weaker. "I—" He stopped. "God has given us all freedom, Katherine. He doesn't control us. Freedom, it's . . . it's a terrible gift. These are hard questions. Easier to answer on paper, I think, than . . . but fair questions. They're fair questions. God didn't fault Job for asking."

"Who's Job?"

Mr. Dodgson looked relieved. "Well, he's a character in the Old Testament who—"

"I haven't had Old Testament yet," I said, cutting him off. "Not till eleventh grade."

"Ah," said Mr. Dodgson.

I squinted at him. In a way, I pitied him. "How can you possibly keep thinking God is so great if you believe he *exists* and he left you guys *alone* while your mother got beaten?"

Mr. Dodgson sighed. "I didn't say he left us alone. I said he didn't *fix* everything. There's a difference. Maybe his revealing himself to Alisa as a lion king is his way of not leaving her alone. Why shouldn't the Lord of the Universe reveal himself to a little girl in whatever manner he chooses?"

I folded my arms across my chest. "Whatever happened to your mother?" I asked, changing the subject. "Is she dead now?"

Mr. Dodgson stood up and began to gather his books together. We were both six or seven minutes late for class by then. "I'm afraid, Katherine, we'll have to continue this after school," he said. "It's gotten late."

I stepped through the doorway into the hall and hesitated, turning back around. I didn't intend to talk with him after school—or ever, if I could help it—but I was curious. "Just tell me," I said. "Is she dead now? Did she get away from your father? Was it okay in the end?"

Mr. Dodgson stood in the doorway, gazing away from me, down the hallway. "She's dead," he said shortly. "She never left my father."

"Oh." I took a step back. And the next thing I said sounds mean, now that I think of it, but I hardly realized I was saying it out loud instead of just thinking it to myself. "See?" I said. "It doesn't help to believe in God. We have to help ourselves."

I know Mr. Dodgson must have heard me, but he didn't answer. He left me standing by his office, and I watched him click down the hall. I realized a few seconds later that I'd forgotten to ask for a hall pass, and that he'd never actually promised to stop calling our house, but I was too tired to go after him. Anyway, I knew what I needed to know.

Mr. Dodgson was a religious fanatic—at the very least—and he was poisoning Alisa's mind. Whether or not he meant any harm, he was our enemy. I could see more clearly than ever that I had to keep him far away from all of us. And most of all, far away from Alisa.

Chapter Sixteen

We had to wait around till nearly five-thirty that evening before Douglas finally made it home from the bank. Tracey and I were on the side steps, smoking. Smoking was about all we ever did anymore. Alisa had arrived home on the school bus two hours earlier and gone straight to her room without speaking to either of us.

The weather was cold and sunny—back to normal for November—and Douglas's face was bright red from exertion when he rode up the driveway on his bike. His hair was sweaty at the edges, and his knuckles were purple from the wind. I automatically thought that I should offer him food because I knew he must be starving. But of course there wasn't anything. We were having the last of the rice with the end of a jar of olives for dinner. Then for breakfast there was half an envelope of instant oatmeal per person. After that, we'd be completely out of food. The refrigerator, the freezer, and the cupboards were empty. There was literally nothing left except food coloring, spices, mousetraps, and a can of Ajax.

I couldn't tell from Douglas's face whether he'd gotten the money or not.

"Well?" I snapped as he climbed off his bike. I couldn't stand not knowing. "Did you cash the check?"

Tracey didn't say anything, but I knew she was as impatient as I was. We'd both been in a terrible mood all afternoon, hardly speaking to each other. Tracey had a headache that she said was ready to split her head open, and aspirin hadn't helped it any.

Douglas pushed his hair out of his face. "Yes and no," he said, gasping for breath.

"What does *that* mean?" I demanded. "Did they give you the money or not?"

"Wait," he said, tossing his bike so it leaned against a hedge. "I need to get some water, and then I'll tell you. It's complicated." His voice was extremely squeaky. He climbed up the stairs past Tracey and me, and we could hear him rummaging through the kitchen cabinets, then thundering water into a glass from the sink in the bathroom. He must have drunk that whole glass in about five seconds, because we heard him filling it again. After the third time, he came back outside, glass in hand. Tracey handed him a cigarette and he took it, panting. There was water on his chin and I noticed he was wheezing.

"You should stop smoking so much," I said automatically.

Douglas didn't answer, but he and Tracey both shot me looks that clearly said "Look who's talking."

"We should all stop," I amended. "As soon as we have food again, I'm quitting. Your chances of cancer go way down if you quit before you're twenty."

They still didn't answer. We were all quiet for a while, as Douglas's breathing slowed back to normal. Tracey suggested that we go up to the tree house, in case Alisa decided to eavesdrop again. "It'll just upset her even more if she hears us talking about the money," she said.

I shook my head. "She's locked in her room still. She's not speaking to us, remember? She won't hear."

Douglas lit his third consecutive cigarette.

"Will you please say something?" Tracey demanded. "Or are you just going to stand there chain-smoking till you have an asthma attack?"

Douglas exhaled. "Okay," he said. His voice was more steady now. "Here's the thing. They let me *deposit* the money. That part went fine."

"Okay," said Tracey, "so the money's there, in the account."

"Yeah. And I asked the lady if I could have a hundred dollars of it in cash. For my mother, who was sick—I told her what you said to say. But the bank lady said I should tell my mother that the check would take one business day to clear . . . and in the meantime, her account is frozen, because it's below the requisite balance."

"What the hell does *that* mean?" I exploded. "How come bank people can't just talk English? If it's our money, how come they won't just give it to us?"

"*Wait,* Katherine," said Douglas. "I know what it means; it's not that bad. It just means that before we put this check in, Mom didn't have a hundred dollars in the account. So they can't give us the cash until they've made sure Dad's check has gone through."

"What if his check doesn't go through?" said Tracey. She looked scared. She looked on the verge of tears, actually.

"There's no reason why it won't," said Douglas sensibly, looking at her. "Dad's a dentist. He's rich. This is a normal thing for banks; it always takes a little while for the check to clear. Sometimes longer than one day, but the lady said since the check was written on the same bank, the money would be there tomorrow."

That was all a little over my head, but it was the kind of thing Douglas always knew, and I trusted him. "Tomorrow," I said quietly.

Douglas nodded. He put his hand briefly on top of Tracey's head and awkwardly ruffled her hair like he was petting a dog. Two tears rolled down her face, and she kind of laughed at the same time, and grabbed another cigarette. "I'm just really hungry," she said, wiping her eyes carefully with her thumbs so her eyeliner wouldn't smear. "Duh," she added, "so is everybody else."

I put my cigarette out slowly, thinking. "It's past dinnertime," I said. "I'll make the rice. We just have to get through one more night and tomorrow morning. We'll make it."

Tracey nodded. "I know." More tears rolled down her face.

"Maybe you should take another aspirin and go lie down."

She nodded again, for once not arguing.

I followed Tracey into the house and watched her go to her room, ready to help her gain entrance if Alisa insisted on keeping the barricade going. But Alisa let her in immediately, then marched to the living room sofa, where she lay mummy-style, her arms folded across her chest, and stared coldly at the ceiling.

I sighed and went to the kitchen. Douglas was already in there, at the table.

"Katherine," he said.

"Uh-huh."

We had just over two cups of rice left in the bag. I poured them into a stack in the middle of the shiniest copper-bottom pot we had. Then I added exactly four cups of water, and shook some pepper in very carefully, watching the patterns it made on the surface of the water. We were all out of salt. It's weird how ritualistic you get about cooking when you don't have enough to eat.

"Something else about the bank . . . ," Douglas said.

"What?"

"Well, I asked if they were open on Saturdays, and they are—till noon, so I'll have to go in the morning. But the lady asked me, 'Doesn't your mother have an ATM card?' "

"A what?"

"An ATM card. You know, a cash card. You put the card in the machine and it gives you cash."

I turned around to look at him. "She does," I said. "She does have one. I've seen her use it before, but I don't . . . Do you know how it works?"

"It's easy," said Douglas. "Except you need the password. Katherine, if we could get the card and figure out the password, we'd be all set till Mom gets better. We'd have access to cash whenever we wanted it. We wouldn't have to worry about food or anything."

I put a lid down over the rice. "That's stealing, Douglas," I said slowly. "I mean, that's *really* stealing. I think using someone else's cash card is, like, a felony."

Douglas exhaled fast and shook his head. He was so sullen those days; he really wasn't like himself at all. "She's our mother, Katherine," he said. "And the check is Dad's. It's *child support.* It's supposed to be our money *anyway.*"

For some reason I was remembering when my mother first taught me to make rice. I must have been about eleven, and she was showing me how to make supper for that night because she had a date with Sheldon. She'd stood behind me at the stove and helped me measure the rice and the water.

Her hands had been over my hands, and she'd smelled like perfume and sugarless gum, and I remember she was wearing this shiny copper bracelet that was brighter than the copper on the pot. It kept clanking against the side of the pot, like music.

"It's still stealing," I said to Douglas. "I'm not saying we shouldn't do it, but I don't exactly want to explain it to Mom when she wakes up."

"Well, what the hell does she *expect* us to do?" snapped Douglas.

I whirled around. "I'm not *saying* we shouldn't *do* it," I practically yelled. "I'm just *saying* it's *stealing.* Okay?"

Douglas leaned back in his chair and looked at me incredulously.

"And I have no *idea* what the hell the stupid password is," I said quietly, turning back to the rice, which didn't need stirring, and smoothing my hair.

"Well, I'm going to look for the card after dinner," said Douglas after a while. He was using his overly reasonable voice again, like he thought he was talking to a lunatic. "And I think we should make a list of words she might have chosen. Or dates—you know, like her birthday. We could try our phone number. People usually choose something uncomplicated, so they'll remember."

"Great," I said, still looking at the pot. "Terrific."

"You know, Katherine, this is probably our only chance at survival. I didn't want to say this in front of Tracey, but that lady at the bank acted really suspicious. They may give me cash tomorrow, if we're lucky, but they won't do it more than once. And there's no way they're going to give me more than fifty dollars without Mom being there in person."

I nodded. "I said, *fine,* Douglas. I'll get the card myself. I have to bring Mom some rice anyway, and you're too clumsy to go in there and get to her purse without waking her up."

Douglas shook his head. "Fine," he said, leaving the kitchen. "Whatever."

I heard him climb the stairs to his room and shut the door. After a while I heard his guitar, and the music sounded angry—not his usual mellow lament.

I turned the heat down under the rice and went to sit at the table with my head down on my arms. The pressure of my arm against my eyelids made Ferris wheels of red beads against the darkness.

After a few minutes I heard a tiny noise and looked up. Alisa was standing right next to me, staring at me. Her hand was resting on the back of my chair. "Are you crying?" she asked.

I shook my head as my eyes readjusted to the light in the kitchen. I wasn't crying—just thinking depressing thoughts, which is what I do instead.

"Tracey's crying," she said.

"Tracey has a headache," I said. "She's hungry."

Alisa nodded. She continued to stare at me steadily.

"I forgive you," she said after a long time. And for some reason that *did* make me want to cry.

"I'm glad," I said.

Alisa climbed up into my lap. She put one arm behind my neck. "I know the word," she said quietly.

"What word?"

She laid her hand lightly on my arm. "The secret word you need. I was with Mommy at the bank when she got it. It's my name."

"Are you sure?"

She put her head down on my shoulder. "It's my name," she said. "It's Alisa."

Chapter Seventeen

The next morning was the longest six hours of my life. Douglas took Mom's ATM card with him and left at six-thirty to deliver his papers. After that, he was going to ride to the bank and, if all went well, be back by eleven with the cash. Tracey, Alisa, and I saved the oatmeal till almost nine-thirty, but when we finally ate, the portions were so small, they were worse than nothing. It was slightly warmer outside, but cloudy and gray, so you couldn't even see the sun moving to prove to yourself that time was passing, and the house was just the level of dark that made it hard to stay awake, but if you turned an inside light on, it didn't seem any brighter.

After a while we drifted away from the table and fell asleep. Tracey went to her room to lie down, I wrapped up in an afghan on the sofa, and Alisa curled up catlike in a living room wing chair. Alisa's hand was in a relaxed fist against her lips, which was how she'd slept ever since she'd stopped sucking her thumb at age five. The television was on, but neither of us was watching, and soon I was so deep asleep I couldn't even hear the raucous music of the cartoons and sugar-cereal commercials.

When I woke up, my hands were stiff and sweaty like I'd been clenching my fists the whole time. Stretching, I looked at the clock and saw that it was almost eleven-fifteen, which made me nervous. I wondered where Douglas was. It probably hadn't been the greatest idea to send him biking miles and miles when he was so hungry. I'd given him a dollar to buy a candy bar at the first gas station he passed so he'd have some calories to burn. Still, thinking about it, I wished I'd given him more.

Alisa was still lying in the same position. Her mouth was open, and her face was flushed with sleep. I blinked heavily and clutched the edges of my afghan. I intended to stay up and wait for Douglas then, but in a few minutes I was asleep again and dreaming.

I dreamed I was standing in the woods, looking out across an open field of snow that stretched uphill all the way to the horizon, scattered with rocks and boulders. It was nighttime and there was a full moon, so the sky looked like a polished shell of navy blue and the snow and rocks were bright under its light. Far away I could see Mr. Dodgson climbing uphill, toward a single lamppost with a gas flame. A few yards behind him, Alisa followed in his tracks, leaving a crumbled trail of snow like powdered sugar.

I was about to go after them when I noticed someone in the shadows just a few feet from me. It was the ice-witch I'd seen on the cover of Alisa's Narnia book. She was leaning against a tree, perfectly still, and watching Alisa and Mr. Dodgson intently. A thin layer of clouds drifted in front of the moon like luminous fish scales, and the witch muttered something in a language I couldn't understand. Then, raising both arms above her head, she broke from the woods and began to run toward Alisa with horrible silent speed—much faster than anyone could really run in snow. It was like watching a spider you think is dead suddenly dart sideways and run up your arm. I shrieked Alisa's name, but my voice bubbled and disappeared, like when you try to scream underwater in a swimming pool.

At the same time, way up near the horizon, a huge shaggy lion stepped into the light cast by the gas lamp. His mane was silver, except where the light turned it gold, and his paws were huge in the snow. I knew he must be Aslan. He turned and looked across the field, past Alisa, Mr. Dodgson, and the witch, and straight into my eyes. Shaking his mane, he opened his mouth and began to roar, and *this* sound didn't disappear. Instead, it grew and reverberated and shook the earth.

When he roared, my blood ran cold. I was more afraid of the lion than of the witch, and I turned around and ran back to the woods as fast as I could, sliding in the snow and tripping over branches to get into the shadows where I could hide. I forgot about everything else—even saving Alisa.

The next time I woke, it was because somebody kept saying my name.

"Katherine . . ."

I was glad to hear it. I thought it was Douglas, home from the bank.

"Katherine, sweetie . . ."

I pulled the afghan tighter around me.

"Katherine . . ."

I opened my eyes and saw my mother standing over me in her nightgown, staring down at me. Her face looked swollen, fat and grotesquely pale. She was swaying back and forth a little bit. Before I could even react, she turned around and half sat, half fell right on top of my legs—like I wasn't even there. With a shock of pain I sat up so fast I saw stars. As I tried to untangle my arms from the afghan, my mother struggled back up and teetered forward, giving me just enough time to jerk my legs free before she sat down again. That time she trapped the edge of the afghan, so I was caught against her in a tangled knot of blanket.

The smell of rot was overwhelming.

"Katherine," she gasped. "Get me some orange juice." Her hands were in front of her on her knees, and her arms were bare under the short sleeves of her nightgown. Her hands were shaking violently.

Across the room, Alisa was sitting straight up in the wing chair, staring at us. Her eyes were large with fear. There was a pink mark where her fist had been against her face, and she was so still she almost didn't look real.

"I'm sick," said my mother. Then she sighed deeply and put her head down on her knees so all her hair fell forward, parting itself into greasy clumps. The sound of her sigh should have filled me with pity, but for some reason it filled me with hatred instead. Partly because her breath was so bad and her hair wasn't beautiful anymore. Partly because Alisa's eyes were so huge across the room. "I need some juice," Mom said, shuddering. She said it to the floor.

My heart was racing and my hands shook as I tried to untangle myself from the blanket without yanking on the part that was under my mother. Awkwardly I got free and managed to pull myself to a standing position. "We don't have any juice," I said, so coldly that it shocked even me.

"I need some," she said, still looking at the floor. "Oh, Tracey. Oh God. I'm so thirsty."

"I'll get you some water," I said more quietly, heading for the kitchen. I hated it when she called me the wrong name.

I took my time filling a glass for her. I had a weird feeling, like it was the middle of the night, but from the microwave clock I could tell I'd only been sleeping a few minutes since the last time I'd woken up. The stars that had come from sitting up too quickly were still buzzing around the edge of my vision like fireflies.

By the time I returned to the living room, I had better control of myself. Alisa had disappeared. My mother took the glass of water and drank about half of it. Then she set it unsteadily on the end table.

"I wanted juice," she said, slurring the *s* sound.

"We'll get you some juice," I said. I picked the glass up automatically and slid a coaster under it. That was ironic; it was my mother's rule never to leave a glass on the table without a coaster. "We're going shopping later," I said. "We'll get some then."

That statement seemed to register in my mom's mind, because for the first time she looked straight at me. I wondered if I'd made a terrible mistake. The last thing we needed was questions from her about *how* we were going shopping, and with what money. But a second look at her face told me she didn't even know who I was.

"Good," was all she said.

I followed her back up to bed, staying just one step below her on the staircase and keeping both my hands on the banister in case she fell backward.

Douglas didn't get home till about an hour later. Tracey, Alisa, and I all watched impatiently as he rode up the driveway.

"Did you get it?" asked Tracey. She didn't even wait for him to get off his bike.

Douglas was purple again from exertion, but he raised his left hand high above his head as he steered with his right and dragged his sneakers across the pavement to slow the bike. At first I thought he was waving, but then in a green-gray flash, I noticed what all of us were by that time desperate to see.

His fist was full of cash.

Not only that, but when he climbed off his bike, he unzipped his backpack and brought out a quart jug of milk and a one-pound bag of M&M's, which he'd bought at the gas station minimart on the way home.

"Look," he said, smiling at me, "I know you said come straight home, but I thought you'd forgive me if I stopped just once." It was the first time I'd seen Douglas smile in days, and I couldn't help smiling back.

"You're late," I said, but so gratefully that he knew what I meant.

We split open the bag of M&M's right there on the front steps and ate the candy in handfuls. Douglas, Tracey, and I passed the milk jug back and forth, swigging out of it like medieval people drank beer out of jugs, and we poured some of it into Alisa's cupped hands because we were too impatient to go inside and get a cup. Alisa laughed when the milk touched her hands, and some of it ended up spilling on the sidewalk, but it didn't matter anymore. We had cash, and if all went well later that night, we'd have groceries too—groceries to spare.

I wasn't afraid of the next part of the plan anymore. I wasn't really afraid of anything. The ten minutes or so that it took us to swallow all that chocolate was probably the most joyful ten minutes of my entire life up till that moment. And it wasn't only the sugar rush from the candy that made me feel better. It was the feeling that if this *was* a war, we were at least in the battle again. We still had a chance.

Chapter Eighteen

Nearly thirteen hours later, at one-fifteen in the morning, a little of that courage had deserted me. My heart was racing. Still, I felt braver than usual.

"Tracey," I said, "Make sure Alisa has her seat belt on tight, will you?"

"She's asleep already," said Tracey from the backseat. "She's all slumped over."

"I don't care," I snapped, twisting around to look at them. "If we crash this car, she's going to go flying through a window whether she's sleeping or not. Get it on her, now! And make sure yours is tight, too."

"I'm not going to crash," muttered Douglas. He was feeling around the ceiling for the interior light switch, and his arm was bent over his head at a weird angle. Finally he found it and snapped it on so the inside of the car was bathed in dim greenish light.

Alisa moaned in protest as Tracey propped her in a sitting position and pulled the seat belt tight around her middle.

Douglas leaned back in the driver's seat and surveyed the

dashboard. He flipped on the headlights, and the hemlock tree in front of the driver's side was suddenly illuminated in an eerie flash. The car was still parked the way my mother had left it the day she'd picked Alisa up at school—at the edge of the driveway almost right on top of the hemlock.

"You better watch out," observed Tracey, "or we'll drag that tree with us when we back down the driveway."

Douglas didn't answer her. He turned the key carefully in the ignition and the windshield wipers and radio came on at the same time, making us all jump. Douglas's hands shook as he felt around for the knob that controlled the volume.

"Douglas," I said for the millionth time, "I can drive if you don't want to. I'm older."

He twisted a switch on his left, and the windshield wipers squeaked to a halt. "I can *do* it," he said. "I've done it before. It's just Jon's car was different."

I was pretty sure Douglas was exaggerating about how much driving he'd done in his life. His friend Jon Wiseman was fourteen, the same age as Douglas—and way too young for a learner's permit in Washington, D.C. To hear Douglas talk, you'd think he and Jon went cruising around the Beltway on a regular basis. I suspected in reality Jon's dad had let them back the car down the driveway and circle the cul-de-sac a couple times. Still, even that put Douglas way ahead of me as far as driving experience was concerned, and I wasn't anxious to get behind the wheel myself, so I didn't argue. We had to get to the supermarket somehow. Even if we could have biked there, we wouldn't have had a way to bring back all the groceries. This was the only logical way.

"I don't know why you made us wait till the middle of the night, Katherine," said Tracey from the back. It had been a long time since we'd eaten the M&M's, and we were all hungry again, and tired.

"The later we go, the fewer people will be there," I said, adjusting the mirror on my side. "It's open twenty-four hours."

"We could have at least gone at, like, ten," muttered Tracey. "I'm sure all the normal people in the world are finished shopping by then."

"The roads are clearer now," I said. "Fewer people to crash into."

"I'm not ging to *crash,*" said Douglas again, flooring the gas pedal with determination. The car revved, coughed, then stalled. That always happened when my mother drove it too. It was an old car.

Alisa moaned in her sleep. It's amazing what little kids can sleep through.

Douglas tried the gas again, and this time the engine coughed twice and caught. The muscles in my throat tightened, and I tugged on the shoulder strap of my seat belt to make sure it was secure. Douglas pulled the gear lever over to the letter R, which he said stood for Reverse.

The car began to roll backward. It made a tearing, crunching sound as it disengaged from the hemlock tree. We rolled down into the street in front of our house and stalled again.

Douglas pulled the gear-thing back to Park and gave it gas again. This time the engine started right away.

"Turn off the interior light, will you, Tracey?" he said.

Tracey snapped it off and I realized she was right beside me, leaning over the seat. She didn't have her seat belt on. I was about to make a comment about that, but Douglas threw the car into Drive, and I forgot what I was going to say. The car lurched forward into the darkness, and we started rolling past the neighbors' houses—most of which were dark and had their shades pulled down securely against the night.

When I think back on the drive now, I can only remember bits and pieces. I remember being very nervous the whole time that Douglas was driving too close to my side of the street, and worrying that he was going to sideswipe one of the cars parked along the edge. I kept saying, "Get over to the left!" but Douglas kept insisting he was already practically over the yellow line on *his* side.

The ramp onto the highway was particularly scary. I think Douglas took the curve too fast, because at one point we all got sucked over to the left by sheer force of gravity, and it felt like the car was going to flip. Then he hit the brakes to compensate, and we slid onto the curb a little before straightening out and edging back onto the road again.

At least there was nobody else on the highway—not for a long way in either direction. The only cars we saw were way over in the left lane. We stayed on the right. Douglas pushed the car faster and faster until the orange needle went up to fifty miles an hour and then stayed there. The speed limit was sixty, but like I said before, the car is old. You could tell it was laboring as hard as it could; it sounded out of breath.

At the grocery store exit, Douglas slowed way down to about five miles an hour. He was being extra cautious after the entrance-ramp mistake, and I was glad. It felt safer. The store was right off the exit, and Douglas stopped and signaled with the blinker before we turned into the parking lot and cut across diagonally to park right under the red neon FLAVE'S SUPERMARKET sign.

There were only four other cars in the lot, and they were all over at the other side. The store was open, though. A big banner in the window said PORK CHOPS 99 CENTS/LB. and right under that it said WE'RE OPEN 24 HOURS A DAY—7 DAYS A WEEK!

We stepped out of the car like the first astronauts stepping out of their spaceship onto the chalky surface of the moon. The wheels rolled backward a little, and Douglas jumped in again to pull on the emergency brake.

Alisa was still sound asleep and slumped over in the backseat.

"Tracey, maybe you should stay out here with Alisa," I said hesitantly.

Tracey just looked at me with that slight lift of her eyebrows.

"We'd better go inside," Douglas said after a minute. "This looks bad—us standing around the parking lot."

I nodded and pulled the back door open. Alisa lifted her head, looking confused.

"Come on," I told her, "we're going shopping."

Bleary-eyed, she climbed out of the car, rubbing her nose.

I held her hand firmly and, keeping her away from the car, slammed the door shut with my foot. Douglas took Alisa's other hand, Tracey walked behind us, and the four of us crossed the empty parking lot to the automatic doors of the supermarket.

Inside the store every aisle was strung with Thanksgiving decorations. Paper pilgrims hung from the ceiling, and giant plastic turkeys with brown tissue-paper tails roosted on top of candy displays. The electric clock on the wall read 1:58, and a Muzak version of "Yesterday" by the Beatles was piping over the stereo system.

"It's weird being the only ones here," observed Douglas.

"We're not the only ones," I said. I could see a redheaded man in a leather jacket down in the ice cream section, and a black woman all wrapped up in colorful scarves rooting around in the pharmacy. Otherwise, though, Douglas was right. The aisles were all waxed, shiny, and empty. A guy about Douglas's age was sitting at the only open cash register, reading a Star Trek novel. Beside him was a little black-and-white TV that kept flashing pictures of different areas of the store—to catch shoplifters, I guessed.

"Okay," I said. "We need to do this fast and get out of here."

"How much money do we have?" Alisa wanted to know.

"Enough," I said, looking at Douglas, who had three hundred dollars in his pocket. "Enough to get pretty much whatever we want. Tracey, can you go get us a cart? I'm trying to think of how to organize this. . . ."

Tracey went and returned with a cart.

"Let's go by food groups," I said finally. "That way, we'll end up with balanced nutrition. Tracey, you and Alisa get all the fruit and vegetables. Douglas, get meat and, like, dinner stuff. I'll get pasta and bread . . . and milk and butter. You should all get baskets from that stack over there, and I'll keep the cart with me. Then we'll meet at the end and figure out what we forgot. Okay?"

They all agreed, and we split up.

When we got back together about half an hour later, we had a lot more stuff than would actually fit in one cart, so we had to get another one. We also had a lot of questionable items: eight quarts of ice cream, for instance, three cartons of cigarettes, a curling iron, several magazines, five or six boxes of Mallomars, and a copy of the *National Enquirer*. Douglas had thrown in a sixteen-pound turkey, which I wasn't sure I'd be able to cook, and Alisa for some reason had dumped in an entire holiday crate of Florida grapefruits.

I made them put back the curling iron, the cigarettes, half

the ice cream, and most of the magazines. Everything else we decided to keep, and after doing one last inventory, we headed for the checkout. The carts were so heavy, it was hard to make them roll in a straight line, especially because one had a wheel that kept turning inward and jamming.

We were almost on top of the black lady with the scarves before I realized she was there, at the checkout. If I'd seen her in time, we definitely would have waited till she was gone. But I'd been distracted by the broken wheel on the cart, and I was trying to do some rough math in my head to make sure we hadn't gone over three hundred dollars. Once we were standing right next to her, we didn't have much choice except to act natural and start unloading the groceries onto the conveyer belt. In the confusion I didn't notice that Alisa had disappeared.

I tried to look casual as I crammed all the rolling grapefruits behind the plastic bar that separated our groceries from the lady's. She had only a bottle of aspirin, NyQuil, cough drops, and a box of Kleenex.

"That'll be eleven dollars and thirty-nine cents, Ms. Haley," said the checkout boy. "I need a driver's license if you're gonna write a check."

Ms. Haley. My blood froze, but I didn't look up. I just turned slightly away from the cash register, pulled two cereal boxes out of the cart, and set them on the belt behind the grapefruits. An envelope of strawberry Pop Rocks slid out from between the boxes and fell to the floor.

I crouched down to pick up the pop rocks, and straightened back up facing away from Ms. Haley. Pretending to yawn, I lifted a *News Pulse* magazine out of the rack and began flipping through the pages. At the same time, I met Douglas's eyes and mouthed, *"Go away,"* hoping he could read my lips.

Douglas didn't ask any questions. He pulled on Tracey's sleeve, and the two of them wordlessly slipped around the corner to hide behind some bookshelves. Meanwhile I kept pretending to be completely engrossed in my magazine. My eyes rested on a picture of a Catholic priest in handcuffs, being led to a squad car parked outside a church. The caption read, "Child abuse scandal plagues small-town Catholic parish—shocks the nation."

"Hey, wait a minute. Ms. Haley?" said the checkout boy. "I just need your telephone number on that."

"You'll find it right there under the signature," said Ms. Haley. Even with her throat stuffed up from a cold, she spoke more distinctly than anyone I've ever known, pronouncing each syllable. That's what made her so intimidating as a principal. Kids could instantly sense that she was a powerful woman. Her kindness didn't come from weakness.

"Oh, sorry," said the boy, sniffing. "I didn't see it there."

I read:

Father Michael Callahan was led from his church today in handcuffs, following allegations of abuse made by several children in his care. Callahan himself has vehemently denied all charges. A spokesman for St. John's is quoted as saying, "The church has suspended judgment until Callahan has been allowed a fair trial. However," he adds, "functionally, in a case like this, we must assume guilt until innocence is proven, in fairness to the alleged victims." Father Callahan was suspended from duties until further notice, and was arrested yesterday afternoon.

"Thanks for shopping at Flave's," said the boy. "Have a good night."

"You have the same," said Ms. Haley, and nodded slightly. Then she turned and nodded in my direction too, almost imperceptibly. I was facing sideways, with my head bowed down over the magazine, and my bangs fell across my face. Ms. Haley hadn't seen me since I was a sixth-grader, and if she recognized me, she didn't show any sign of it. She just tucked her grocery bag under her arm and, holding her head very straight, walked out of the store. I wondered how I had failed to recognize her even all the way across the store. Her walk was very distinctive. Dignified.

"Cash or charge?" asked the checkout guy, looking at me.

I blinked and lowered the *News Pulse* magazine a little. "Huh?"

"Cash or charge?"

"Oh," I said, stuffing the magazine back in the rack. "Cash. Just a minute." I squeezed past the cart and stuck my head around the corner. "Douglas!" I hissed. "Come back."

All three of them came back. They were white.

"Did she know who you were?" asked Alisa, wide-eyed.

"Paper or plastic?" asked the guy.

"No." I shook my head. "I don't think so."

"What was she doing here in the middle of the night?" Douglas said. "It's two A.M."

"I guess she has a cold," I said. "She probably lives near here."

"Paper or plastic?" said the guy again, sticking his hands on his hips. You'd have thought there was a long line of people behind us, from his attitude.

"Paper," said Douglas. "It's better for the environment."

"No," I told the guy. "Plastic."

"Can I stand in the cart?" asked Alisa.

"If we get plastic, we can use them later for trash bags," I said to Douglas, lifting Alisa into the mostly empty cart. She knelt down at one side and started handing me armfuls of food to put on the conveyer belt.

A few more unauthorized items went past me that I hadn't noticed before. Ding Dongs. A Kermit the Frog notebook. Hair elastics. But all of a sudden, it really *felt* like two-thirty in the morning, and I decided not to put up a fight.

The total came to $263.47. Douglas handed the guy two hundred-dollar bills and four twenties.

"Thanks for shopping at Flave's," said the guy, after he'd counted out our change. He didn't sound like he meant it, though.

He gave us a really weird look as we went out the door.

Chapter Nineteen

Our main worry after that, of course, was whether or not Ms. Haley had recognized us in the supermarket. If she had, we knew she'd definitely tell Mr. Dodgson and we'd hear about it soon. But the last few hours of Saturday night passed in silence; our phone never rang. Sunday morning we slept late. When I woke up, I checked our answering machine for messages, just in case, but there weren't any. After the clock struck two, we started to relax. We figured their church service had to be long over with by then, so if Ms. Haley had talked to Mr. Dodgson, we would have heard from one of them already. We decided once and for all that Ms. Haley *hadn't* recognized us, and we spent the rest of the afternoon and evening in peace.

It was more than peace, actually. The whole day was blissful. It was like one long victory celebration that got happier and happier as we were more and more sure we hadn't been caught. From the moment we'd pulled into the driveway the night before, we'd felt like the champions of the universe. Douglas had noticed as he parked the car that the gas needle was on Empty, which only made the whole shopping trip seem like more of a miracle—like maybe we'd gotten to the market and back on sheer willpower, without any gas at all.

The fact that we had plenty of groceries and cash lent a totally new atmosphere to the house. The refrigerator, freezer, cupboards, and fruit bowls were all full. Sunday afternoon we did laundry, vacuumed the whole house, and replaced all the light bulbs that had burned out. Even though we couldn't fix the big things like the kitchen sink and the thermostat, the house seemed warmer and safer. I brought my mother a plate with crackers and hot soup and left it on her night table with two glasses—one of juice and one of ginger ale. She drank all the juice and half the ginger ale, and actually said, "Thank you," before she went back to sleep.

Sunday night, even though we'd been eating all day, we decided to make a feast to officially celebrate the fact that we weren't busted. We considered cooking the turkey and having Thanksgiving dinner a week early, but I read the directions and it turned out that a turkey takes almost three days just to defrost. We had macaroni and cheese instead, with salad and garlic bread, and we all had our favorite drinks—Tracey and I had diet Coke, Douglas had a milk shake with mint chocolate-chip ice cream, and Alisa had strawberry milk. We poured the drinks into Mom's fancy wine goblets, said a toast to victory, and clanked our glasses together. For dessert, we ate a whole box of Mallomars. We had actually pulled it off. Nobody even wanted a cigarette, we were so happy.

Then Monday came, and the whole thing was shot to hell.

* * *

I'd been so confident that our secret was safe, I didn't even worry when Mr. Dodgson called me to his office after class. I figured he just wanted to talk about something else.

It was obvious after he shut the office door, though, that he knew. His face was red with anger.

"I don't have time to talk," I said quickly, still standing. "I have to catch the bus."

From the look on his face, I expected him to start shouting at me, but he crossed the room silently and sat down at his desk in his usual dignified way. He looked down at the desk for a minute, and when he started to talk his voice was deadly quiet, and his eyes were like stone.

"Sit down," he said.

I stayed standing for a minute, but the anger on his face deepened and I decided this wasn't the thing to argue over, so I sat.

"Listen," I said, "I really have to go. I can't—"

Mr. Dodgson held up one hand and cut me off. "I spoke with Ms. Haley at evening service last night. She says she saw you, Douglas, and Tracey at Flave's Supermarket on Saturday night at two in the morning. Is this true?"

I hadn't prepared an answer to such a direct question. I couldn't think of what to say.

"Is it true?" he repeated.

"Yes, sir," I said finally, trying to sound unruffled. "We were shopping."

"You were shopping," he repeated. "By yourselves. At two in the morning."

"Yes, we were shopping. What's wrong with that? It's not illegal to shop."

"At two in the morning."

"Ms. *Haley* was there," I argued.

"Ms. Haley is an adult."

So am I, I wanted to say, but I bit my tongue.

"And where was Alisa during all this?" asked Mr. Dodgson.

"She was . . . home."

"And how did the three of you *get* to the supermarket at two in the morning?"

"We walked."

"At two in the morning," he said, "you walked through the city to Flave's. What is it . . . five or six miles from your house to the supermarket?"

"Well, we took the bus part of the way. And then . . . we walked the rest."

"Ah," said Mr. Dodgson, folding his hands. "I didn't realize the buses ran so late."

I didn't say anything. My hands were in my lap, clasped together so they wouldn't shake.

"Whose car was it you drove away in, then?" asked Mr. Dodgson.

"What?"

"Whose car did you drive out of the parking lot? Ms. Haley waited a few minutes, because she was justifiably curious as to who you were with. She mentioned seeing you get in a car, with Douglas driving. She mentioned a small child with you as well. Four of you in all. She watched you drive away in a car—a green station wagon. I'm wondering whose car it was."

I squeezed my hands together tighter. "We didn't drive," I said. "She must have seen someone else. Or else she was lying."

Mr. Dodgson's brown eyes flashed behind his glasses. "No, Katherine," he said quietly. "No . . . she wasn't lying. Miriam Haley is not a woman who lies. I believe she saw exactly what she said she saw. What she didn't know was that Douglas is only fourteen years old. If she'd been aware of that, she would certainly have stopped you."

The clock ticked loudly in the quiet office. I tried to keep my face expressionless and my eyes on Mr. Dodgson, because I knew if I looked away, I'd seem guilty.

He shook his head slowly. "No, Katherine," he said again, "I believe you're the one who's lying."

I didn't answer—just kept squeezing my hands together tighter and tighter. My muscles were practically trembling from some emotion that wasn't exactly fear. More like disbelief.

"I'll tell you what else I believe," Mr. Dodgson continued, getting up and coming around the desk to stand right above me. "I believe you lied to me about your father helping you. I don't believe anyone's helping you at all. I believe you are four children trying to run a house by yourself with no help from any adults, and that you're failing miserably. Your mother is drunk. You're desperate, and you're making foolish decisions that are putting both your own life and the lives of your siblings in danger. And I believe it has to stop."

I stood up quickly and backed toward the door, sliding the chair in front of me as a barrier. My heart was beating way too fast. I didn't want to panic, but at that moment it was hard not to, because I just couldn't think of a good lie.

"We didn't have any food," I said. "I'm just trying to take care of them." My eyes searched the walls frantically and came to rest on the Narnia calendar that Alisa had colored . . . it seemed like much longer than a month ago.

"And do you call this taking care of them?" said Mr. Dodgson sharply. He looked furious. Still, he hadn't raised his voice. "Hiding your eight-year-old sister under the bleachers in the gym? Driving illegally on the highway in the middle of the night?"

"Douglas knows how to drive."

"Douglas is a fourteen-year-old boy."

"So?" I demanded. "He's not a child."

Mr. Dodgson shook his head. He turned around and began gathering his things together. "He *is* a child," he said quietly. "And so are Tracey and Alisa, and so are you. I see all this now, far more clearly than I did before. I apologize, Katherine; I should have made up my mind more quickly. My hesitation has only made things harder for everyone."

"What do you mean?" I demanded. My heart pounded even faster. "Hesitation about what? You've made up your mind about what?"

Mr. Dodgson shook his head again. He snapped his briefcase shut and took his coat off the back of his chair. "Something has to be done about your situation," he said. "It's my responsibility as your teacher to see that this doesn't continue."

"What are you going to do?"

He put on his coat. "I don't know yet. I'll be speaking with Ms. Haley again tonight. In the meantime, you have a school bus to catch."

My head was spinning. "You can't just tell everyone," I said. "This is my private information. This is my life."

Mr. Dodgson looked sad but resolved. "I'm sorry, Katherine," he said. "The best thing for you to do now is just go home. And for heaven's sake, stay off the road."

I stepped in front of the door to block his path. "Mr. Dodgson," I said. "Wait, please . . ."

He sighed. It was Mr. Dodgson who couldn't look at *me* now, I noticed. That scared me more than anything had so far.

"Please," I stammered. "For Alisa's sake, you can't tell everyone. They'll tell DSS. They'll put Alisa in a foster home. We don't have any other relatives or anything, besides my dad . . . and I was telling the truth about Alisa not having a father. You *can't* tell." The more I talked, the more I sounded like I was begging. I *was* begging. I hated myself for it, but I couldn't think of anything else to do.

Mr. Dodgson reached for the doorknob and I stepped out of his way, out into the hallway, which was full of student noise—people slamming their lockers shut and running and laughing.

"Go home, Katherine," he said shortly. "There's nothing else to say right now. Go catch your bus." He locked his office door, then turned away from me without another word and walked briskly down the hall toward the teachers' lounge, disappearing around the corner. As I watched him go, I felt my face turn red, and I almost started crying from helpless rage right there in the hallway. Me, who never cries.

And then all of a sudden, with a terrible sense of calmness, I knew what I had to do. It came to me all at once—almost like somebody shined the idea into my brain with a slide projector. A picture-perfect plan took shape in my mind right there in the hallway outside his office, and became clearer and more focused as I found my way to my locker, gathered up my books, and rode home on the school bus in a seat by myself, thinking.

I could write a letter.

If I couldn't stop Mr. Dodgson from telling the whole world about my mother, I could at least try to stop people from believing what he said. The *News Pulse* article at the supermarket, which had seemed insignificant at the time, suddenly seemed like it had been thrown into my hands by the powers of fate. I remembered the photograph of the priest being led from his church in handcuffs. He'd actually looked sort of like Mr. Dodgson—not his features, exactly, but the way he seemed to be stumbling along, not sure which way to look.

I could write an anonymous letter to the school administration and make . . . what was it the article had called them? "Allegations."

I curled up on the school-bus seat, thinking.

No, it wouldn't even have to be that extreme. I wouldn't have to actually *accuse* Mr. Dodgson of doing anything. I could just hint that maybe . . . *maybe* he was one of those sick weirdos like that priest. Based on his friendship with Alisa. His . . . unhealthy *interest* in Alisa.

I thought about Marcus Schmidt, the dean of St. Agnes, and how paranoid he was about scandal. I remembered what Sara had told us about Ms. Bledsoe, and how she got fired just for being pregnant without being married. "The school board was afraid of a scandal," Sara had said, "so they just made up some excuse to fire her." I shivered. A pregnant religion teacher was nothing compared to a religion teacher who might be a potential child abuser.

The note began to take shape in my head. I'd print in capital letters—very neatly, so they couldn't recognize my handwriting.

To Whom It May Concern . . .

No.

To Marcus Schmidt, Dean of Students, and the board of St. Agnes Episcopal School:

This is an extremely important matter which needs to be brought to someone's attention. Mr. Dodgson, the new 7th, 8th, and 10th grade religion teacher, keeps calling my house all the time.

That was true, wasn't it? And really, it was hardly appropriate.

> In addition to being very weird and nervous in class, he has called my house and talked to my eight-year-old sister several times on the telephone. This interest seems unhealthy, and makes me extremely alarmed. I think the school administration should look into it and make sure Mr. Dodgson isn't a child abuser like that priest who is currently in the news. (See the latest issue of *News Pulse* magazine.) I would appreciate it if this would happen immediately.
>
> Sincerely,
> A Concerned Tenth-Grader

That was all it would probably take. What had the church spokesman said in the article? "Functionally, in a case like this, we must assume guilt until innocence is proven, in fairness to the alleged victims."

Thinking about it made me feel cold, and I pulled my legs up underneath me, tucking my skirt in around the edges of my legs. There was a freezing draft coming through the windowpane and it almost looked like snow outside. It was too early for snow.

They wouldn't arrest Mr. Dodgson, of course. He *wasn't* a child abuser—really the farthest thing from it—and if they looked into it they'd surely see that. But in the meantime, they might suspend him from teaching. At least they'd take him less seriously if he was going around making accusations about other people.

Maybe he'll get fired.

The thought came to me, and I pushed it quickly out of my head. *He won't,* I told myself. *He almost definitely won't.*

And so what if he does? I reminded myself how just half an hour before, Mr. Dodgson had walked away from me in the hallway, without even the common courtesy of telling me what he was going to do. And here I was feeling sorry for him. He didn't have any sympathy for *us*—for my mother, or me or Tracey or Douglas, whose lives he was about to ruin. Not only that, he was brainwashing Alisa into thinking that Aslan and Narnia were real. He was lying to her, brainwashing her into his religion. That could be a form of abuse.

The bus rolled up in front of my house, and I heard the squeak of the doors opening before I even realized it was my stop.

He's a horrible teacher anyway, I told myself on my way up the driveway. *He'd be better off with another career. He breaks into a sweat just talking in front of groups. Why does he even* have *a career where you have to talk constantly?*

Inside the house, I went straight upstairs, sat down at my desk, and wrote the letter to Dean Schmidt before I could lose my nerve. Then I folded it, put it in an envelope, and sealed it shut. I wrote on the front of the envelope, *Attention: Mr. Marcus Schmidt, Dean of Students. URGENT!*

It's for Alisa's sake, I thought. What was that proverb people always quoted? "All's fair in love and war." *Sometimes in a war, you have to kill the enemies before they kill you.*

I opened my bedroom window and lit a cigarette, leaning into the cold outside air to exhale. *It's too bad,* I told myself. *Too bad for Mr. Dodgson. But that's just the way it is.*

Chapter Twenty

The next day it started to snow. The ground wasn't cold enough for the flakes to stick, but they drifted all day against an eerie dark sky and turned to mush on the grass and to dark splotches on the street. St. Agnes and St. Luke's had a half day of classes because of teacher meetings; I was just as glad because that meant I didn't have to face Mr. Dodgson. Right before I left on the bus at noon, I slipped the letter into Dean Schmidt's in-box as planned. I hadn't told Tracey and Douglas about the letter, or even about the confrontation the day before. It wasn't that I felt guilty exactly—I just didn't want to waste all my energy trying to explain it to them, and I didn't want to ruin the mood in the house.

The atmosphere had dulled a little, but it was still pretty festive. When we got home from the half day, Tracey, Douglas, and I all congregated in the kitchen, which had become our new hangout. In a way, it was weird how fixated on food we were, but on the other hand it wasn't too hard to figure out. We'd just stopped taking it for granted.

Tracey set six yogurts and the cookie jar on the table, then returned to the refrigerator for milk. "That's weird," she said when she opened the door. "The refrigerator light isn't working."

"Maybe it's a fuse," said Douglas, with his mouth full of cookies. "I'll look at it after we eat."

Tracey flipped the light switch on. "This doesn't work either," she said. "It can't be the bulb—we just replaced it."

"I'll look at it after we eat," Douglas repeated, and cookie crumbs blew out of his mouth as he talked.

I rolled my eyes at Douglas and walked over to the living room, taking my yogurt with me. "The lights in here don't work either," I said slowly, flipping the switch on and off, then checking the plugs in the wall. "If it was a fuse, it would just be one room, right? These are all out too." When I stopped to think about it, I didn't hear the refrigerator humming either. Everything seemed unnaturally quiet.

I looked back at them, and I think we all realized the truth at the same time. Only Douglas said it out loud, though. "She didn't pay the electric bill," he said.

From where I was standing in the living room, I could see the stack of mail in the foyer. It had been accumulating for more than two months. "I'm sure she hasn't paid *any* of the bills," I said. "But why would they just shut it off like that? Why now? I mean, what if our *heat* were electric? It's *snowing* outside."

"We must have passed some kind of deadline," said Tracey.

"Well, still," I said, irritated, "isn't that illegal? It should be illegal just to shut it *off*." The snow seemed like it was coming down harder, the whole house felt gloomy, and all of a sudden I really wanted the lights on.

Then we heard a terrible crash.

It thundered right over our heads—so loud that the walls shook. At first I thought there'd been an explosion or something—something to do with the electricity being gone. But it was followed by a horrible, muffled screaming sound like an animal moaning.

We stared at each other, paralyzed.

"It's Mom," said Tracey.

Somehow, Tracey's voice was the thing that unfroze my feet. I ran up the stairs two at a time with Tracey and Douglas right behind me. I pounded on my mother's bedroom door. It was shut and locked. I rattled the doorknob, but it didn't give.

"Mommy?" I called.

The upstairs hallway has no windows, so without lights on it was as dark as a tomb outside her door—and silent.

"You guys," I barked to Tracey and Douglas, "get a flashlight or something. I can't see." My voice was shaking. I dropped to my knees to search for the bobby pin under the carpet, but my hands were shaking too, and I couldn't find it. Tracey and Douglas scrambled back down the stairs together, and inside the room I could hear my mother moaning again. After what seemed like at least five minutes of groping around, my fingers finally closed around the bobby pin. I stood back up, felt the doorknob with my other hand, and managed to pop the lock.

The door swung open. My mother's bed was full of light, but it was empty. Then I saw her body in a dark heap in the bathroom doorway, and when I looked at her, my mind registered only the color red. Red stains on the nightgown, red-brown sherry on the carpet, red blood squirting everywhere in her hair and onto the floor, like a fountain.

I stepped back out of her bedroom, and that weird calmness came over me again—the kind that takes all my nervous energy and just sort of ties it in a knot.

Douglas and Tracey were at the top of the staircase with a flashlight. "I don't need that anymore," I told them. "Turn around and go downstairs. And stay there." They went without asking questions.

I called an ambulance from the phone in my bedroom, looked at the clock, and noted that Alisa's school bus wasn't due for another two hours. Then I wet a washcloth with cold water and went back to my mother. She was lying a few feet away from where she'd fallen; in the middle of the floor. I knelt beside her, holding the washcloth against her forehead and murmuring "I love you." I just kept saying it over and over again: "I love you, I love you, I love you . . ."

She pushed at me with her flabby white arms, trying to get the washcloth off her face. "Gedoffemeh," she slurred. Her face and hair were sticky with blood, which was still spurting from a two-inch gash above her left eye. As I pressed the cloth against her head, my arms and throat convulsed. I couldn't help it. There was vomit all over her chin and neck, and the toilet in her bathroom was all stopped up, overflowing onto the carpet. Direct pressure wasn't stopping her bleeding; the blood was soaking right through the cloth. And there was shattered glass everywhere.

The bleeding didn't stop until much later. She bled and bled, unaware of anything that was going on, while the ambulance men took her pulse and asked her their rude questions. "Are you intoxicated, ma'am? Ma'am—how much liquor have you drunk today?" They were so rough and loud, I couldn't believe they were trained to work with sick people.

One of them asked me, "What's your mother's name?"

"Suzanne Donavan," I said uncertainly, shrinking back against the wall. Their loudness terrified me. Everything had been so quiet in our house for so long.

"Suzanne!" they shouted, shining a flashlight right in her face. "Suzanne? Ma'am? Sue? How much liquor have you drunk today? Have you taken anything else? Look at me, Sue. What's your name? What day is today?"

No one ever called my mother Sue. I could have told them that, but once they'd gotten her name, they acted like I wasn't even there anymore.

She was still dazed and unresponsive when they strapped her to a metal stretcher. She didn't hear me on the telephone to Hawaii, leaving a message on my father's voice mail at the hotel, asking him to call me at the hospital with my mom's insurance number ASAP. She didn't hear my harsh directions to Tracey and Douglas—to clean up the blood on the stairs, to shut Mom's bedroom door, to make sure Alisa didn't see any blood or glass, and to keep things under control until I got home. She was unaware that the neighbors were staring at us from their driveways as the men wheeled her stretcher down the walk in broad daylight and snow flurried down from the sky. She probably didn't notice that I lied to the EMT about my age so I could accompany her in the ambulance. She just bled and bled. Occasionally, she clawed drunkenly at the air.

She didn't seem coherent at all until much later—at least three hours later—in a little cubicle near the emergency room. By that time she had five stitches above her eye, and the whole side of her face was swollen grotesquely, like the Elephant Man. I'd stood with her in the confusion and pain of the emergency room for what seemed like days and days. I'd held her hand during the electric hum of the X rays and helped the harried-looking technician coerce her to lie still. Then I'd sat with her in the same blindingly white room for eons, listening to the clock tick and watching her while she slept.

She woke up once. She seemed to notice I was there, but she didn't have anything to say. She just lay there and stared at the IV tube running from her arm up to a sack above her head. When anyone else walked into the room, she closed her eyes.

After we'd been there at least two hours, a nurse walked in with a message from my father. On a yellow sticky note was scrawled my mother's social security number, the name of the insurance company, and my father's full name. That was all.

"I was going to come get you," the nurse said, "but he couldn't stay on the line. He just told me the numbers." She glanced back at the note. "He's a doctor, huh? Maybe he couldn't get away. I know how that is."

I realized she was trying to be kind, so I said, "Yeah."

"Does he practice in Hawaii?"

"No," I said. "He's just on vacation there. He practices in Michigan."

Then I added, "A *dental* practice." Because I wanted the nurse to know that there wasn't any emergency that could have kept him from staying on the line. "He's a *dentist,*" I said again, and I hoped she got the point that the only reason he didn't wait to talk to me or even find out why his former wife was in the hospital, was that he was a worm. A dirt-eating worm, just like my mother always said.

A nervous-looking doctor came an hour later with a mousy-looking woman twice his age. He introduced the woman as a hospital chaplain. She was wearing a fire-engine-red sweater vest and a big beady gold cross, and she said she'd come to help and see how my mother and I were feeling.

I ignored the chaplain and stared at the doctor. Glancing down at some scrawls on his clipboard, he told me that my mother's blood alcohol level was back below the legal limit, and that her head would heal within a couple of weeks. The stitches were the kind that dissolve into the skin and don't need to be removed surgically, so she wouldn't have to return to the hospital. Did I have any questions?

I said I didn't.

The chaplain's eyebrows shot up.

The doctor went on to say that he *strongly* recommended my mother check into the hospital's detox program. He couldn't commit her forcibly, and he'd already discussed it with her but she'd refused, and "with human rights and all" he couldn't really do anything. His words all ran together, like he was making this speech for the five hundredth time that day. He probably was, for all I knew.

"Katherine?" my mother murmured from the bed. We all looked over at her. She started to sit up, but when she saw there were other people in the room she closed her eyes and sank back down into the pillow.

"Can we go home now?" I asked the doctor.

"She doesn't need to stay from a medical standpoint," he said. "And she's refusing treatment for substance abuse. I'll have a nurse come unhook the IV in a few minutes. You'll need to sign some forms at the checkout desk on your way out."

"Thanks."

He nodded quickly and left. The chaplain didn't show any signs of following him, which annoyed me.

"Perhaps when things have settled down, you could get together with your father or another relative, and *confront* your mother about what's happened today," she said to my back as I started gathering Mom's things. "Alcoholics can't be helped unless they're willing to help themselves. Group intervention often works wonders, however."

I turned to glare at her and she pinned me with her eyes, fingering her sweater vest. I realized that she wasn't a mouse. The doctor had been a mouse. This chaplain was a hawk in a mouse disguise.

"Who are you going to call to drive you home today?" she asked, looking very interested.

For a minute I considered telling her that my father was busy cavorting around Hawaii in a Jaguar with another woman and couldn't even be bothered to return a simple phone call. Furthermore, we didn't have any other relatives that I knew of—except a crazy pot grower in California. "I'm it," I wanted to say. "I'm all she has. And I lied to the EMT earlier—I'm not eighteen, I'm fifteen. Barely." But I realized the chaplain might have an answer for that. She was probably a spy from the hospital, wanting me to say *exactly* that so she could have an excuse to legally lock my mother up and put us all in foster homes on the spot.

"I'm going to call a taxi," I said and, thinking quickly, added, ". . . to go to my grandparents' house. I called them before, and they want me and my mom to come stay with them for a while on the farm. So my mom can get better."

The chaplain pursed her lips and skewered me with her eyes. She knew I was lying, I could tell. But she didn't seem to have any power to stop me from leaving—maybe because of the human rights laws the doctor had mentioned earlier.

"Thanks for all your help," I said. "Could you please tell a nurse we need this IV out of my mom's arm? You could just mention it on your way out. Thanks. Goodbye."

The chaplain shook her head slowly. To my surprise, she left without another word.

I was pretty sure she'd be back soon, so I turned to my mother and helped her sit up. "Come on," I said. "We're leaving as soon as they unhook you. I'll get a taxi."

My mother seemed a little groggy still, but she understood me. I was pretty sure she'd listened to the whole conversation. She'd only been pretending to sleep.

"Good girl, Katherine," she said under her breath. Her face was still all swollen and there was a cut on her lip, so I couldn't tell whether her words were slurred from that or the liquor. She swung her legs around the side of the bed and stretched out her blood-encrusted hands toward me. "Do me a favor, will you?" she said. "Get some paper towels from the bathroom? Wash the blood off my fingers?"

She looked tragic and stupid, and my throat closed up.

"Fine," I said, and hurried out the door.

Chapter Twenty-one

My mother didn't talk during the ride back to our house. I figured she was just waiting to get home so she could get drunk again and go back to bed. The taxi driver was an old black man with bloodshot eyes. He smoked the whole way, and he didn't have anything to say either, so it was a quiet ride—all of us staring out different car windows at the snow that must have fallen while we were inside the hospital. It was dark by that time, and the temperature had dropped. The snow was raining down in white sleety sheets, sticking to the street in irregular patches. I could only remember one other time in my life when we'd had snow before Thanksgiving, and that was way back when my father used to live with us and Alisa wasn't born yet. A thousand years ago.

I shut my eyes for the rest of the drive and rested my forehead against the glass, trying not to think.

I'd almost forgotten about the electric bill until the taxi pulled up to our house and the windowpanes were dark. It looked weird—the house all wrapped in gloom and snow pouring down diagonally from the sky. The lawn was white. It was so strange I started to shiver.

"Fourteen dollars," said the driver.

While I handed him the cash, my mother climbed out of the taxi and staggered across the front lawn toward the house. I figured out the tip in a hurry and ran after her.

The front door was locked. My mother rang the doorbell but it didn't work. She pushed it again, and a third time, swearing.

"The electricity is off," I said, reaching past her to bang on the door with the knocker. Behind us the taxi backed out of the driveway, leaving black tracks in the snow. The car's headlights made white triangles in the darkness, like in a cartoon drawing, and I suddenly felt sorry to see the driver go, even though he'd been so surly. At least he was an adult.

I heard footsteps inside the house, and after a minute Douglas and Tracey opened the door, looking scared. Douglas was holding the lantern from the tree house. Its yellow light flickered everywhere like a cheerful explosion. The light seemed out of place against everything else. It gave me back a little of my courage.

'Hi," I said.

My mother didn't say anything. She pushed past Tracey and Douglas like she didn't recognize them and headed unsteadily to the kitchen. I squeezed Tracey's arm and followed my mother.

"Katherine," said Douglas in a low voice. He was right behind me. The lantern swung in his hands and threw crazy shadows every which way. "Why didn't you call from the hospital? We have to talk."

"In a minute," I told him. "Mom? Be careful—the lights aren't working. What do you need? Why don't you go to bed and I'll get it for you?"

My mother seemed to know her way in the dark. She went straight for the pantry, pulled out a rectangular bottle of vodka, and set it on the counter with a clacking sound. She got herself a glass.

"What's wrong with her face?" asked Tracey, who'd hung back a little. "Is she all right?"

"She's fine," I said, and crossed the room to stand beside my mother. "Mom, you shouldn't drink right now. Please. They said the alcohol in your blood was too high. Can't you just . . . at least take a break?"

"Katherine," said Douglas again. He set the lantern on the kitchen table, and the light steadied.

I shook my head impatiently. "Not now. Mom, *please.*"

My mother acted like she didn't even hear me. Lifting the bottle of vodka, she balanced the neck on the lip of her glass and let the liquor pour till it overflowed. Then she picked up the glass with both hands like a child and gulped it down like she was drinking milk. She tipped her head back till the glass was empty. When she was finished, she set the glass down again and walked out of the kitchen, swaying slightly, with absolutely no expression on her face. She looked like a zombie.

My mouth dropped open a little and I started to go after her, but Douglas caught my sleeve.

"Stay here, Katherine," he said. "I *have* to tell you something."

"What?" I said, jerking my arm out of his grasp and watching anxiously as my mother climbed the stairs. "Did you guys vacuum the stairs and in her room and stuff? I don't want her stepping on any broken glass." The last thing I wanted was to go back to the emergency room. The bones in my arms and legs were literally aching—from stress, probably.

"Katherine, *listen,*" said Tracey. "We picked up all the glass. Listen to Douglas."

"What, then? Tell me—hurry up!" I heard my mother's door shut and the creak of springs as she fell into bed, so I relaxed a little.

"Alisa is gone," said Douglas.

I turned around to look at him. "What do you mean, gone?" I said slowly. "Gone where?"

"Gone. *Lost.*" said Douglas, jamming his hands in his pockets. "We haven't seen her since four."

"Four o'clock this afternoon?"

Douglas nodded.

I shook my head, confused. "But it's practically nine-thirty now."

"Yeah," he said. "I know."

"Well, where *is* she?" I said, trying to stay reasonable. "That was more than five hours ago!"

"We've looked everywhere we could think of," Douglas said in a flat voice. "We can't find her. She's not in the tree house, or anywhere around here. As soon as she heard that Mom was in the hospital, she just bolted out the front door and took off running.

"You told her Mom was in the hospital?" I echoed incredulously. "You *told* her what happened?" I stomped my foot in frustration. "Douglas, how *could* you?"

He pushed his hair out of his face and looked at the floor.

"How come you didn't just *chase* her?" I could hear my voice getting shriller and shriller, as the meaning of his words absorbed into my brain. "She's been gone since four? She could be kidnapped—or dead! Douglas, she could be anywhere! It's dark outside. It's *snowing.*"

In the doorway, Tracey started to cry. She didn't make any noise, but tears started rolling down her cheeks faster and faster. She turned around and walked away from the circle of lamplight into the dark.

"Katherine," Douglas pleaded, meeting my eyes, "it's not my fault. What *else* was I supposed to tell her?"

"Anything!" I was almost screaming. "You could have told her anything—something creative. Anything but that! How can you be so damn stupid? How hard is it to keep track of an eight-year-old? Do I have to do everything by myself?"

Douglas didn't answer. He stayed where he was, turning whiter and whiter, with his hands jammed down in his pockets.

"Did you look all over, in the yard and stuff?" I said after a little while. My heart was pounding. "You're sure she's not in the house somewhere asleep? It's so damn dark in here, she could be practically on top of you and you wouldn't know."

"We looked everywhere," he said, hardly above a whisper. "She's gone. She just took off. We thought she'd come right back, but she didn't."

I stared at him, unbelieving. Then I turned around and kicked a chair as hard as I could. It flew across the kitchen and fell over on its side with a crash, making Douglas jump.

It's too much. *This is too much.* That's what I wanted to say. I wanted to scream it.

Instead I said, "I can't believe I trusted you, Douglas. I hope you're proud of yourself."

He flinched visibly, and I didn't feel sorry at all. I felt glad.

I crossed the kitchen to where our jackets were hanging and pulled on Douglas's heavy winter coat and some boots. "I'm leaving," I said. "I'm going to look for her."

Douglas followed me to the door. "We already looked

everywhere around here," he said again. "Maybe we should just call the police."

"No," I said fiercely, turning around and glaring at him. "No. Don't you *dare* call the police."

He stepped back like I'd slapped him. "Do you want me to come with you?"

"*No.* Stay here and try not to screw anything else up. I'll find her."

I slammed the door in his face and went out into the snow by myself.

We live, technically, in the suburbs, but very close to Washington, D.C., so it's always partially light outside at night—especially when it's cloudy. The clouds catch the lights from the city and glow with an orange tint. They were glowing that night, so I could see clearly except for the snowflakes pouring down sideways and making me dizzy. I pulled the hood of Douglas's jacket up over my head and tightened the drawstrings.

I decided to check the tree house first, since that was the most obvious hiding place. Douglas had said they'd checked earlier, but I thought Alisa might have gone somewhere else first and doubled back since then. If she was angry at us or too scared to come inside, she might have gone up to the tree house to avoid the snow. I think I really believed she'd be there, because it wasn't until I'd climbed the ladder, lifted the trapdoor, and looked around at the empty shadows that I started to panic.

I felt around the tree house floor till I found a pack of cigarettes and a lighter and stuffed them in my coat pocket. Then I climbed back down the ladder and stood there under the shelter of the tree, smoking and trying to think clearly.

Where else would she be?

Alisa had plenty of friends at school, but they lived scattered all over the neighborhood, and I doubted she would have gone to any of their houses. Especially in the last year, she'd been less interested in her playmates than she was in her books.

The thought of books made me wonder, suddenly, if she might have headed for the library. That was five blocks away—technically within walking distance, although Alisa wasn't allowed to go by herself. They closed at four on Fridays, but she might not have remembered that.

I threw my cigarette down in the snow and headed for the library.

Oh God, I whispered as I walked, *please let her be safe. Please don't let her be killed or kidnapped.* When I'd gone about three blocks, I had a horrible vision of Alisa being carried into the same emergency room where I'd just spent the evening, and I started to run.

A series of pictures flashed through my mind while I ran. I saw Alisa as a newborn baby, home from the hospital and wrapped in a hand-me-down baby blanket. My mother had just finished nursing her, and I was sitting on the living room floor holding her in my lap. Her head was so fragile and small, it could rest completely cradled in one of my hands.

Then I remembered when Alisa was a little older—two or three. Mom didn't have time to date as much in those days, and she'd sometimes sit with us after supper and tell us stories. Most often she told us about the night Dad had left, and how she'd felt she "couldn't go on." Those were the exact words she always used. She'd be drinking, with Alisa cuddled in her lap, and the rest of us around the kitchen table in our pajamas, hanging on her every word. "I'd been a housewife all those years," she'd explain, "with three children aged three, four, and five, and he just . . . *left.* How could I go on? I had a string of affairs . . ."

"With who?" we'd ask, eyes wide with horror and sympathy.

"Oh, I can't even remember. But after a year of it, I was at the end. I had actually decided that I was going to *take my own life.* But then—presto, pregnant." She'd laugh bitterly into her sherry. "And there were two lives to think about."

Five, I'd correct her silently, automatically.

"And nine months later, Alisa was born." She always cheered up at that part of the story. "My little saving angel from heaven." She'd hug Alisa tightly and smile at the rest of us, and Alisa would lean close into her neck and her honey-colored hair. Alisa never minded the smell of sherry.

Once when Alisa was three, I'd heard her whisper into Mom's neck, "I won't let you die," and for a split second I'd wondered if she really was an angel. But my mom didn't hear Alisa. She just kissed her and handed her to me to put to bed, and I knew then, from the smell of spit-up on Alisa's sleeper and the wheezing way she breathed, that she was just an ordinary three-year-old kid.

When I reached the front gate of the library, I was panting and my lungs ached horribly, so I stopped to lean on the wall and catch my breath while I scanned the front of the building for any sign of Alisa. The library is the oldest building in our neighborhood. It's a brown stone building that looks like it came from a story itself, and it's completely surrounded by a stone wall. In the snow that night it looked surreal. Floodlights by the front steps lit the whole building like a fairy-tale castle. There was no noise, no movement anywhere, and no footprints in the snow.

Please, I prayed again. I walked all the way around the

building, checking the doorways and porches. The inside lights were all off, and I could see the red electric eye of the burglar alarm. A pay phone glowed eerily at one side of the front porch. Paper announcements thumbtacked to the outside bulletin board fluttered in the breeze, and one came off and blew into the snow, bouncing down the front steps.

There was nobody there.

I sat down on the steps for a minute, resting my head on my knees and listening to the snowflakes fall on the back of my hood.

I remembered Alisa swinging on the rope swing in our backyard—her red sweater brilliant against the green lawn. I remembered her crouching down at Tracey's feet on the school bus to St. Agnes, pushing her stringy hair out of her face and smiling at me. I remembered her drawing pictures on the sidewalk with a crab apple, and how scared she'd been to show me the letter from her teacher that day—the letter that said she'd run away from school, looking for the door to Narnia.

I lifted my head. All of a sudden I knew where she was.

Digging in my pockets, I was relieved to find change among the cigarette paraphernalia and other garbage. I took out two quarters and lifted the receiver off the pay phone. The first quarter, I used for Information. The second, I used to dial Mr. Dodgson. I hesitated before I dialed the last four digits, remembering the letter I'd dropped in Dean Schmidt's in-box earlier that day. But then I thought, *It's too early for him to know about that,* and I forced myself to hurry up and finish.

Mr. Dodgson answered on the first ring. "Hello?"

His voice threw me off, and for a second I didn't answer. I looked around at the snow.

"Hello? . . . Hello?"

What if Alisa's hurt?

I cleared my throat, and pushed my voice out hard so it wouldn't falter. "Mr. Dodgson?" I said.

"Yes. Who is it?"

"It's Katherine Graham," I said.

There was a pause on the other end of the line and I got scared that he was going to hang up. I started to stammer. "I—I'm sorry to call you, but . . . "

I wrapped the phone cord around my fingers. "Something happened. Alisa's lost, and there's no one to look for her. She's been gone for a long time. Please, I need a car. Don't hang up. Can you come get me?"

There was another pause, and I heard him clear his throat. "What's happened, Katherine?" he said. "I'm listening. Try to speak a little more slowly."

"Alisa's *lost,*" I said again, and the reality of it hit me with full force. I squeezed the phone cord around my fingers so tightly it almost cut off my circulation. "I think she may really be in trouble. I need your help."

There was static on the other end, and I could hear him moving around. "Where are your parents now?" he asked quietly.

"My dad's in Hawaii. And my mom's . . . hurt. We had to go to the hospital today." I put my hand over my eyes and squeezed them shut. "Please," I said. "There's no one else to help. I need a car."

"Okay, Katherine," said Mr. Dodgson. He sounded sorry. "Certainly . . . certainly I'll come. Can you give me directions to your house from the Beltway?"

"I'm not at my house," I said. "I'm outside the Buker Memorial Library. You know where that is?"

There was another pause. "I know where it is," he said. "Stay there. I'll come get you as soon as I can."

"Thanks," I said. "Can you bring a flashlight with you?"

Mr. Dodgson sighed. "I'll do my best," he said.

"Okay."

I hung up the phone and sat down on the steps to wait, watching the snow pile up slowly on the stone.

Chapter Twenty-two

It took Mr. Dodgson about forty-five minutes to get there, which was longer than I'd expected. When he finally arrived, we didn't say much to each other. I just climbed into his car, shivering. I gave him directions and he drove, taking the turns cautiously because of the snow. It was mostly slush on the road, and I could feel the car sliding a little whenever he applied the brakes.

"Go left here," I said after we'd been driving about ten minutes, "and find a parking place near the elementary school. We'll have to walk the rest of the way."

Mr. Dodgson put his turn signal on and waited for a snowplow to pass us in the darkness. Then we swung into a parking place by the school's side doors and he turned off the engine. "Could Alisa have made it this far on foot?" he asked doubtfully.

"Alisa is a very determined person," I said.

Mr. Dodgson made a noise in his throat that I couldn't exactly interpret.

"Did you bring a flashlight?" I asked.

He pulled one from the floor behind his seat. It was about as long as a baseball bat, with a red siren-looking thing on one side.

"That's a flashlight?"

"This is my dear sister-in law's *idea* of a flashlight," he said, pulling a wool hat over his head and handing me a scarf. "She sent one to me and each of my brothers this past Christmas, along with cellular phones, road flares, and jumper cables."

"Oh," I said. It had never occurred to me that Mr. Dodgson had brothers and an extended family. "Well, if it works, we'll need it. I think Alisa may be over in the woods behind the school. That's where she said she saw the door to Narnia before."

"Why would she be here now?" Mr. Dodgson asked as we climbed out of the car and started jogging toward the edge of the playground, where the woods were.

"She's looking for Aslan. You know; you're the one who told me. She thinks if she can get to Narnia and find Aslan, he'll cure my mother."

"But at this hour? Why tonight?" Mr. Dodgson started huffing and puffing even before I did, so we had to slow down and walk.

"Because," I said, "my mom fell down and had to go to the hospital—which Douglas, like an idiot, *told* her."

"Douglas is a truthful young man," said Mr. Dodgson, breathing heavily.

"Douglas is totally missing the gene for survival," I said. "If he didn't have me to protect him, he'd be dead."

"Ah," said Mr. Dodgson.

We reached the wire fence at the edge of the woods, and Mr. Dodgson shined his flashlight into the darkness. I started to remember all the stories I'd heard about those woods during my elementary-school years. The teachers all used to say they were full of drug dealers, but the kids thought they were full of ghosts.

"Alisa?" I shouted.

The only sound was the snow falling on the trees and the muffled traffic noise from the streets wrapped all around us.

Mr. Dodgson tried. "Alisa!" he shouted. His voice carried farther. "Alisa? If you're back there anywhere, yell!"

We stopped and listened, but we didn't hear anything.

"Alisa!" I tried again.

Mr. Dodgson paused to look at his flashlight. "Hmmm," he said. He hit a switch on the end, and all of a sudden the red siren came alive, honking and wailing. We both jumped, and Mr. Dodgson fumbled frantically for the switch. He couldn't find it, and finally he thwacked the flashlight against the fence to shut it off. There was a small tinkling of glass as the siren attachment shattered.

And another sound, a voice at the same high pitch as the tinkling glass.

"Katherine!"

I heard it before Mr. Dodgson did, and straining my ears, turned toward the farthest part of the woods, where it came from.

"Katherine? Help me!"

That time Mr. Dodgson heard it too. "Alisa?" he called. "Where are you? Keep shouting."

But we didn't hear her voice again after that. I grabbed the light from Mr. Dodgson and shined it through the fence, squinting forward. I couldn't see anything in the snow, so I threw the light back at Mr. Dodgson and climbed over the fence, dropping down into a puddle of slushy water on the other side. "Shine it that way, okay?" I told him, pointing. "I think her voice was coming from over there. I'm going to look."

I was ready to run on by myself, but to my amazement Mr. Dodgson began to climb the fence too. "Wait," he huffed. "It's dangerous."

I could easily have left him behind in the time it took him to get over the fence, but I suddenly didn't want to. I had no idea what I was going to find in the woods, and I decided I'd rather have Mr. Dodgson with me than go alone.

He splashed heavily to the ground beside me, and stood there catching his breath. "Here," he panted. "Hold on to the light."

I took it from him and waited while he rested. I was surprised he was so out of breath, because I wasn't, and I'm fat too. I decided it must be worse to be old and fat than young and fat.

"Okay," he said. "Which way?"

I shined the light in the direction where I'd heard her voice. There wasn't much snow on the ground because of the trees overhead, but the undergrowth was tangled and filled with icy puddles. We had to walk slowly. Mr. Dodgson stepped on an empty beer can, which made a loud crunching sound and a pop.

"Alisa?" I called again, and we stopped and listened for several seconds before we heard her voice again—a low, muffled wailing.

Moving forward through the trees, we crossed a stream, which we didn't see until we'd stepped in it up to our ankles. That slowed Mr. Dodgson down, and I ran ahead, shining the light behind me so he could still see. Pushing back a thick curtain of pine needles, I stepped into a tiny clearing where there was less undergrowth and more light.

When my eyes adjusted, I saw Alisa huddled at the foot of a tree so loaded with ice that the top of it bowed to the ground in an arch. Except for her breathing between sobs, she was perfectly still.

"Alisa!"

I dropped the flashlight in the snow.

Alisa didn't move. She didn't even turn her eyes toward me. I didn't know what to do. I was so afraid she was hurt or paralyzed or something that I couldn't even go over to her and find out. My heart beat faster and faster and I just stood there like an idiot.

There was a crashing noise behind me then, and Mr. Dodgson stepped into the clearing.

He hurried to Alisa's side, took off his coat, and spread it over her like a blanket. Then, leaning over, he gently scooped her up in his arms, coat and all. She sobbed louder when he did that, but she wrapped her arms around his neck and buried her face in his chest, so at least I knew she wasn't paralyzed.

"Shhh," he whispered, "we're going home."

To me he said sharply, "Take the flashlight. Walk in front of me. We have to get her to the car where it's warm."

Pushing myself to move, I picked up the flashlight and led the way back to the fence, stumbling a little over the branches and trying to point out the puddles to Mr. Dodgson, while Alisa cried in such a miserable way that I could hardly stand it.

Looking back on it, I think I was a little delirious myself by that time. I hadn't gotten much sleep the night before, and my brain kept skipping back and forth crazily between pictures, like right before you fall asleep. First I'd see the emergency room, then our pitch-dark house, then Dean Schmidt's in-box, and then the woods again. Douglas's coat wasn't really waterproof, so by that time I was soaked and my teeth were chattering constantly, which in itself can make you feel pretty insane.

I'm not sure what would have happened if I'd gone into those woods alone. I might not have come back. As it was, the only thing that kept me going was concentrating on holding the flashlight. Mr. Dodgson wasn't too coordinated under the best of circumstances, but holding Alisa made it even harder for him to maneuver his way through the woods, so it was slow going. After a while Alisa's sobbing subsided to occasional hiccups, and the only sounds in the darkness were the crunch of our footsteps and Mr. Dodgson's labored breathing.

Back at the car we sat Alisa down in the front seat and turned on the heat full force so her legs could get warm. Mr. Dodgson sat in the driver's seat, revving the engine and adjusting dials on the temperature panel. I climbed into the back where I knelt and propped my elbows on the vinyl seat that divided me from Alisa.

She was still wrapped in Mr. Dodgson's coat, and she'd stopped crying.

I couldn't stop shivering. "Alisa," I said, hardly above a whisper, "did someone do something to you? I mean . . . did someone hurt you back there?"

Mr. Dodgson shot me a warning look, but I'd already seen Alisa start to shake her head, so I ignored him and kept talking. "Why were you crying, then? Because you were lost?"

"I wasn't lost," said Alisa, leaning her head against the window. Her voice sounded tired and wavery—but stubborn as always. "I wasn't *lost.* I knew where I was. I went there to find Aslan." She shut her eyes.

The car was starting to warm up, and everyone's teeth gradually stopped chattering.

"So you were crying because Aslan didn't come," suggested Mr. Dodgson after a while. His voice was quiet.

Alisa turned to look at Mr. Dodgson, and I saw tears roll down her face. Obviously he'd hit a nerve. "No," she said loudly. "*No.* He *came.*" She wiped her tears away with her fist. "Of course he *came.* Why wouldn't he? I was right there at the door."

My stomach tightened.

"Okay," said Mr. Dodgson. "You don't have to talk right now, Alisa. Just get warm."

But Alisa sat up straighter. "Aslan said I couldn't *go* to Narnia," she said bitterly. "He came to the door, but he wouldn't let me in. He told me to go back home." She folded her arms and tears streamed down her cheeks. "And it kept snowing and I was so cold . . . I couldn't get back over the fence."

"The fence?" I echoed, grasping for reality. "You couldn't climb back over it? How did you get over the first time?"

"It was easy the first time," she said, shrugging, and wiping her cheek with an impatient swipe of her palm. "But going back I was tired, and my sneakers were all slippery." She leaned against the car door again, suddenly tired. "I knew if I went back to the Narnia door and waited, you'd come."

I digested that. I almost hadn't come. I hadn't come for hours.

Alisa looked at Mr. Dodgson again. "How come Aslan made me go home?" she demanded. "All those other children went, in the books. I'm not too old—I'm only eight. I needed his help!"

I shuddered and pulled off Douglas's coat because the

snow had melted, leaving it soaking wet, which was worse than nothing. Throwing it on the floor, I leaned my head on the seat in front of me and shut my eyes. The pictures were starting again. My mother in the emergency room, with dried blood all over her hands. The library in the snow, like a fairy-tale castle. The oil lantern on the kitchen table, and the look on Douglas's face when I slammed the door in his face. The wire fence at the playground, and a forest full of ghosts.

Too much, I thought.

I heard Mr. Dodgson sigh deeply. "I don't know for sure, Alisa," he said. "No one understands what Aslan does, completely. You should know that from your Narnia books."

I didn't hear any response from Alisa. Water droplets were running down my scalp and dripping on my shoulders. The heat from the vents seemed to be blowing around the ceiling, but it wasn't getting as far as the backseat. I kept my eyes shut.

"I can only guess," he continued after a while, "that Aslan made you come back because your family needs you. You're right that you're still young enough for Narnia. But Katherine, Tracey, and Douglas aren't. Aslan is as concerned with them as he is with you. It wouldn't be *fair* to take you to Narnia and leave them all here, would it?" Mr. Dodgson's voice was grave. He wasn't patronizing her, as far as I could tell—he was speaking with level frankness, as if to another adult.

I shivered again, and wrapped my arms tighter under my ribs.

"He should have made sure I got home safe, at least," Alisa said with a little less venom.

"He knew we were coming," said Mr. Dodgson reasonably.

"I wanted a cure for my mother."

"I know," said Mr. Dodgson. "And he didn't give you one. Sometimes Aslan asks us to bear hard things. It was the same for all the children in the stories."

That seemed to make sense to Alisa, because she didn't argue anymore. For a few minutes the car was so quiet, I could hear the snow falling on the roof over the hum of the heater.

I sneezed loudly.

Mr. Dodgson thumped the dashboard. "We need to get home now," he said. "We need to get you both some dry clothes." He crunched the gearshift into reverse. The car groaned and began to move, rolling cautiously out of the parking place.

"Put your seat belt on, Alisa," I murmured, sinking into the backseat to fasten my own. The seat belt was really only an excuse to move away from their conversation and shrink back where I could close my eyes and try not to see pictures of Alisa curled up in the snow, crying, or of the priest in *News Pulse* magazine being led away in handcuffs. I just concentrated on the feeling of the car gliding through the snow, and tried to make my mind go blank.

When we pulled up to my house, I was hardly surprised to see lights blazing in all the windows. A car I didn't recognize was parked in the driveway. Mr. Dodgson had called DSS, I supposed.

I stared at the house, not unbuckling my seat belt. *Of course he called DSS,* I told myself. *What did you think?* It occurred to me that that was probably the reason it had taken him so long to show up at the library.

"Katherine," said Mr. Dodgson, "don't panic. Miriam

Haley is here. She's going to spend the night with you, to make sure Alisa is all right."

I didn't answer him. Alisa was asleep in the front seat, so she didn't move. I kept looking out the window at the lights.

"Katherine," he said gently, "go on inside. I can't stay, but Ms. Haley knows you're tired. She won't badger you with questions." He shook Alisa's arm lightly, and she jerked her head up, looking confused. Her hair had dried funny and was sticking up like straw. "Alisa, wake up," he said. "Go inside with Katherine now. Get warm."

Alisa stretched, turned, and sank down into the seat, closing her eyes again.

The thing of it was, we were busted. Ms. Haley had obviously come straight to the house, which meant she'd walked in on pitch darkness and my drunk mother passed out upstairs with contusions all over her face.

Poor Douglas, I thought. I wondered what he'd done when Ms. Haley had knocked on the door.

If DSS didn't know everything already, they would soon. There were laws about it, and if Mr. Dodgson had been willing to bend them, I knew Ms. Haley wouldn't. *Teachers have to call DSS if they even suspect child abuse . . .* That first meeting in the tree house seemed like a million years ago. *Drinking too much and not feeding your kids counts as child abuse.*

"Listen," I said. "Mr. Dodgson, I have something to tell you."

"Katherine. Now is probably not the best time—"

"No," I said. "It's important." I twisted the seat belt in my hands while I talked. "I think Dean Schmidt may get a letter saying . . . well, *implying* bad things about you—things that aren't true."

He didn't answer, and I wasn't sure whether he understood me or not.

"So listen," I said. I couldn't get the priest in handcuffs out of my mind, and I was beginning to feel frantic. "The letter—it may get you in some trouble. It's kind of a harsh letter. It's anonymous. But I can be a witness to say that it isn't true. Okay? If Dean Schmidt says something, just find me and I'll take care of it."

Mr. Dodgson stayed silent. He looked out the windshield at the snow.

"Do you get what I'm saying?" I asked. My face was starting to feel hot.

Mr. Dodgson sighed. "This letter is anonymous?"

"Yes. Well, no. I wrote it."

He turned to look at me. I wasn't sure how to handle that, so I squirmed around and looked out the window.

"I know about the letter, Katherine," he said.

That took me off guard, and I looked back at him.

"It's a very serious matter," he said. "Dean Schmidt contacted me immediately when he received it. He needed to give me fair warning, as they've scheduled an administrative meeting tomorrow to discuss it. And also," he added, "he wanted to caution me—not to have any contact with you or your siblings before then. On penalty of immediate dismissal."

I stared at him. "How?" I stammered. "How could *he* know? The letter was anonymous. How could he know it was from me?"

Mr. Dodgson smiled sadly. "Not many students at St. Agnes have an eight-year-old sister. Of those who do, only you have served ten hours of detention in my classroom over the last three months. It wasn't hard to deduce."

"Well," I said, faltering, "if Dean Schmidt knows it was

from me, then he must know the letter was a lie. I'll tell him it was. It doesn't matter anymore anyway."

Mr. Dodgson shook his head. "Marcus Schmidt obeys the letter of the law," he said. "The school dictates that any such allegation be followed up by a meeting with the student, the teacher, a representative from Social Services, and an attorney representing St. Agnes." He pulled a letter from his shirt pocket and let it fall on the front seat. "It's all in here, I'm afraid. On St. Agnes letterhead."

I stared at the folded letter. Attached, I could see a photocopy of the letter I'd written. My own meticulous handwriting glared back at me.

"There've been many cases like this—in places similar to St. Agnes." Mr. Dodgson's voice was calm and patient, like he was explaining a concept in religion class. "Rumors of scandal can ruin a school—even if the charges are unfounded. I appreciate your offer of help, Katherine, but you may find that insinuations like these are not easy to take back. Marcus Schmidt . . . well, Dean Schmidt and I have had a number of differences since September. I won't be surprised if they ask for my resignation tomorrow. I'm afraid it's created a lot of trouble for you as well."

I didn't say anything for a long time. The silence wasn't even that awkward, because there was obviously nothing for me to say. What do you say when you've just probably ruined somebody's career, and your own life is shot to hell besides, and the reason for it all—a piece of paper with your perfect handwriting all over it—is lying right on the seat in front of you?

"The meeting's tomorrow?" I said finally. "That meeting you were talking about with the lawyer and everyone?"

"Tomorrow morning at nine-thirty," he said. "They want

it resolved before the Thanksgiving break. I imagine they'll come get you out of class."

"When I called you from the library . . . " My mind was beginning to reel. "You knew I'd written the letter. But you came anyway."

Mr. Dodgson didn't answer.

"Dean Schmidt told you you'd lose your job, if you saw us? But you came to help Alisa."

Alisa moaned in her sleep. One of her legs stretched out and crunched the letter. She sat up, scowling.

Mr. Dodgson patted her foot. "I came for *all* of you," he said shortly. "Now, enough. Take Alisa inside and try to get some rest." He looked away, but I saw in the window's reflection that his face was full of pity. "Go on. It's late. Ms. Haley can help you with Alisa."

I nodded and climbed out of the car without speaking to him again. Alisa tumbled blearily out of the front seat, still wrapped in Mr. Dodgson's coat, and I held her hand as we walked toward the house.

It had stopped snowing. Ms. Haley was waiting at the door, and we didn't look back.

Chapter Twenty-three

We live in Grand Rapids now, with my father and Ophelia. They ended their vacation a week early to meet us at the airport—all of us, including Alisa. They said we could stay with them as long as we needed to. I know I should feel grateful for that.

I'm still trying.

Living here is weird. When we first arrived eight months ago, my father acted really strange around us—like we were terminally ill or something. He kept appearing in doorways when we didn't know he'd been standing there, and asking us stuff like were we comfortable in our new bedrooms, did we want anything special from the grocery store, did we have any medical allergies they should be aware of, was there anything we needed money for? We kept saying no, no, no, thank you, and I had to fight the constant desire to slam the door in his face and lock it tight.

The third night we were in Michigan he came to the room I shared with Tracey, cleared his throat loudly, and asked if he could come in. I said yes. I guessed I didn't really have any choice, considering it was his house.

He entered—just barely—and leaned against the dresser by the door. "How, uh . . . how are you kids doing?" he asked.

I set my teeth and tried as hard as I could not to sound hostile. "Fine," I answered, for the three hundredth time. "We're doing great. It's very nice of you to let us stay here."

He scuffed his feet on the mauve wall-to-wall carpeting. "It was Ophelia, you know, who insisted that you come. And bring Alissa—"

"A-*leez*-a."

"Right. Alisa." He laughed and kind of squirmed at the same time, looking at the floor. "Alisa seems like a nice girl."

"She is," I said. I wished he would get to his point and leave. I'd had a headache for three days, and I wanted to go to bed.

"Listen, Katherine." He glanced up at me for a second and then looked back at the carpet. "I won't be very long. I, uh . . . I just want to say, I know I haven't been the greatest father to you guys in the past."

I stared at him without answering.

"I guess that's obvious," he said, shifting from one foot to the other. "I guess you and Tracey and Douglas kind of remind me of *my* past, you know? And how difficult it was living with your mom. These last few years, Ophelia and I have worked hard to make a new beginning. With the kids and my practice and buying this house . . . Well, we've been under a lot of stress. It's hard for me to think about your mother. Or anything even connected with your mother."

Like her children, I thought, remembering how I'd waited

and waited for his telephone call in the emergency room—and the yellow sticky-note that came instead.

He paused, and I still didn't respond. I didn't know what he expected me to say. *Sorry for your stressful life?* If he thought this speech was supposed to make me forget the events of the past ten years, he was crazy.

"Well." He raked his hand through his hair like Douglas does. "Anyway," he said, "I guess what I'm trying to say is I'm sorry, Katherine. I really am. I hope you guys will be happy here—for as long as you need to stay."

"Thanks," I said. "Now, if you don't mind, I'd really like to go to sleep." I hadn't meant for it to, but my voice sounded angry. Really angry.

My father winced and his eyes met mine. "You know," he said, "it's not easy being an adult, either, Katherine. It's not easy having responsibility for a whole family like this."

I folded my arms. "Yeah," I said, "I know." I could feel my face was hard as stone.

My father sighed. He looked like he was going to say something else, but after looking at my face, he changed his mind, turned around, and walked out instead.

I crossed the carpet to the doorway and slammed the door so hard it sounded like a gunshot, and all the walls shook.

I don't know what the hell he thought. That I was suddenly going to be nice to him after he'd totally stabbed my mother in the back and neglected us for ten years? That wasn't exactly the way life worked. You couldn't go around betraying people—trashing their whole lives—and expect them to love you and treat you like you'd never done a thing wrong.

Except that was what Mr. Dodgson had done.

* * *

The meeting at St. Agnes had been a disaster. It was exactly as bad as Mr. Dodgson had said it would be. Everyone he'd warned me about was there—Dean Schmidt, a blond social worker lady from DSS, and a bored-looking attorney who kept getting paged on his beeper and leaving. They sent Mr. Dodgson out of the room before I arrived, and as soon as I sat down, the social worker started firing questions at me about my family—questions that everyone knew the answers to already, because Ms. Haley had already told them. I tried over and over again to explain that my letter about Mr. Dodgson was a stupid lie, but they wouldn't stay on the subject.

"Katherine," said the social worker, "we hear what you're saying. What concerns us is why you would about-face so quickly in your opinion of Mr. Dodgson between then and now."

"I told you," I said. "I was lying. And I didn't know him as well then."

"Do you know him better now than you did two days ago?"

"Yes. No." It was a trick question. I wasn't sure whether Ms. Haley had told them about Mr. Dodgson rescuing Alisa in the woods or not. There was a long silence as they all watched me, and I knew that either way I answered, I might ruin everything.

Dean Schmidt leaned forward in his chair. "Katherine," he said in a very firm voice, "have you had contact with Mr. Dodgson *since* you wrote this letter?"

I didn't answer. No *or* yes would have been better than nothing, but I hesitated too long and the silence answered for me.

Dean Schmidt blew air through his teeth, the lawyer scribbled notes, and I knew right then it was over for Mr.

Dodgson. No matter what I did, they were going to ask for his resignation, and anything I said was only going to make it worse.

It's been a long, hot summer in Michigan. It may have been Ophelia who wanted us here in the first place, but now that we've arrived, she doesn't exactly act like she enjoys having three teenagers and a nine-year-old suddenly living in her house. I don't blame her. The house is big enough—it's practically a mansion—but it's set up for little kids. Chandler is only three, and Miranda's a toddler. Ophelia is a militant antismoker, so Douglas and I have had to go underground. Tracey quit completely. She never liked it much anyway, and I guess the night Ms. Haley stayed at our house, she told Tracey in graphic detail about her brother's death from lung cancer. Tracey said it was unbelievably disgusting and sad. She and Ms. Haley are practically pen pals now—they write back and forth all the time.

My Dad and Ophelia go to a progressive church where they listen to Native American hymns and have sermons on topics like civil rights and recycling. They've been wanting us to come ever since we moved out here. We've been trying hard to get along with them better, so we finally agreed to go two weeks ago. We all crammed into one pew—my dad, Ophelia, Chandler, Miranda, Douglas, Tracey, Alisa, and me. We sat there nicely, trying to pay attention, and at the end of the service this lady in the pew in front of us turned around and said something about us being "just like the Brady Bunch." She laughed and said my dad and Ophelia must be "working up great karma by taking us all in."

Well, that just about sent me over the edge. I almost opened my mouth and told the lady a few things about my dad and Ophelia's new "Brady Bunch" family—like that unlike the Bradys, we still had a mother in Washington, D.C., who was in a halfway house overcoming alcohol addiction and depression. Furthermore, if the lady thought Dad and Ophelia were doing such a good deed by taking us in, I'd like to know where the hell she thought they'd been for the last ten years, and how this sudden act of generosity was supposed to swing their "karma" so far over the neutral mark. Then I thought of Mr. Dodgson again, and I stopped myself. I didn't say anything. I think Ophelia must have known how hard that was, because on our way out of church she squeezed my hand as a kind of thank-you.

School starts in three weeks, and I think that's just as well. Tracey, Douglas, and I will be going to public high school here—grades nine, ten, and eleven. We missed spring semester, but the curriculum at St. Agnes and St. Luke's was a year ahead anyway, so we don't have to stay back. That's one good thing about living in Michigan—no more private school or stupid uniforms.

There are other good things too; I don't mean to be ungrateful. Chandler and Miranda are cute. When we first came, I thought they were a little *too* cute, but they're starting to grow on me—especially Chandler. He's a very serious kid who walks around with his hands on his hips all the time, worrying about things. I wrote a whole page about him in my green notebook, in a separate section from my list of facts that are true about life. (Solid facts don't seem as easy to come by lately, so I am trying an experiment and writing a documentary journal instead.)

The page on Chandler was really more like a story. A true story. It happened yesterday morning. My father was out in the backyard working on a tree house he's building for the little kids. (It's a lot like the one we had at our old house in Washington, but bigger.) Chandler was out there with his hands on his hips, watching my dad hammer the house together. He looked worried as usual. He wanted to know what the tree house was made out of.

"Wood," said my father, banging a bolt with the side of a hammer.

"Oh," said Chandler. He looked more worried than ever. After a minute or so, he stuck his hands in his pockets and walked back inside, frowning. My father wondered why he'd left.

I could have told him why. At breakfast Ophelia had been reading Chandler the story of the three little pigs—where the wolf huffs and puffs and blows the wooden house to bits, while only the brick house survives. My dad was right there at the breakfast table too, but he'd never make the connection in a million years. I thought it was hilarious, personally. I bet Chandler grows up to be just like Douglas. I think it's funny, Ophelia and my dad having such uptight children when they're supposedly so liberal and laid-back. I like Chandler.

Later yesterday afternoon it got too hot for my father to work, so he came inside to shower and lie down. Alisa and I went out to check on the progress he was making with the tree house.

"It's good," Alisa commented, looking up at the half-finished frame. "It looks like ours at home."

I nodded.

"The yard was better in Washington, though," she added. "It had more trees."

I nodded again.

"I miss Mommy," she said, reaching for my hand.

I didn't say anything, because I wasn't sure whether I missed my mother or not, and I didn't want to say it if I didn't mean it.

My mother didn't stop drinking until they actually took her to the hospital. Ms. Haley took her, and I think the only reason Mom agreed to go at all was because she was still drunk, and she wanted Ms. Haley to leave her alone. Once she signed in, she had to stay for two weeks in detox, and after that she voluntarily checked into a residential treatment center to be treated for depression. As far as I know she hasn't gotten any less depressed, and it's been eight months. She sent us a postcard right after she moved. It said that any contact with us would hinder her treatment, but maybe someday when she got better, we could all be together. In the meantime, she loved us and she hoped we were having fun with our father.

I wouldn't call it fun, exactly, but we're surviving.

Alisa sat down under the tree house where there was a patch of shade. My dad had cut the lawn earlier, and it was perfectly smooth like a carpet, except for stubborn patches of dandelion stems, decapitated by the mower. The stalks stood up straight, darker green than the grass, and pulverized dandelion fluff lay in clumps everywhere.

I sat down beside Alisa and we looked back at the house.

"Katherine," said Alisa, "you still don't believe in Narnia, do you?"

I leaned back on the lawn and sighed. "No," I said.

"Do you believe in God?"

Stretching out on my back, I looked up through the tree branches to the sky. Wind blew through the tops of the tree and jostled the leaves a little. I didn't answer.

"Do you?"

I was thinking about Mr. Dodgson. We'd heard from Ms. Haley that he'd moved to Boston to finish his dissertation, and had applied for a job teaching history at a community college. "I don't know," I said.

"I do," she said, stoutly. "*I* believe in God."

That made me smile. I reached over and squeezed her hand. "Yeah, well, you believe in *everything.*"

"Katherine?"

"Yeah?"

"I have something important to tell you."

I sat up on my elbows and looked at her.

"I'm glad Aslan wouldn't let me into Narnia that night I was so cold. I know now why he wouldn't."

"Why?" I said, pulling bits of dandelion from my hair.

"Because if I'd gone through the door to Narnia . . . I would have wanted to stay there. I wouldn't have wanted to come back."

I pictured how still she'd looked the night she'd run away, huddled at the foot of the tree in the snow. I shuddered.

"Aslan knew you needed me here," said Alisa, pushing sweat-damp strands of hair back from her face. "He knew we needed to stay together as a family."

A breeze blew across the yard, smelling like cut grass and some neighbor's barbecue.

"Well," I said, "I'm glad. I'm glad Aslan sent you back to us." Right at that moment, looking at Alisa's suntanned face, I felt practically joyful. I'm not sure why, even, but I was happier than I'd been in a long time.